AUBADE

AUBADE

KENNETH MARTIN

GMP

First published in October 1957 by Chapman and Hall
First published as a Gay Modern Classic in February 1989 by
GMP Publishers Ltd, PO Box 247, London N17 9QR

©Kenneth Martin 1957
Introduction© Kenneth Martin 1989

British Library Cataloguing in Publication Data

Martin, Kenneth, 1939-
Aubade.
I. Title
823'914

ISBN 0 85449 097 3

Cover art: Detail from Robin and Mate 1954
by Peter Samuelson

Distributed in North America by Alyson Publications Inc
40 Plympton Street
Boston, MA 02118, USA
Printed in the European Community
by Nørhaven A/S, Viborg, Denmark

Introduction by the Author

I wrote *Aubade* in five weeks the summer I left school, and finished it six weeks before my seventeenth birthday – 1000 words a day in three- or four-hour sessions, seven days a week. These days I'm happy to complete 600 words a day, five days a week, whether it's fiction or non-fiction. I wrote then with a purity of purpose and an intense, unquestioning use of my skills that I may never equal. I changed hardly a word as I wrote the first draft on typing paper, cramming the pages from edge to edge with crooked, mostly uphill lines of my small handwriting. With an important exception, nothing was changed in the second draft, which consisted only of copying the book onto lined paper so that a typist could read it. But as I copied I had to change "I" to "Paul" or "he" in the first part of the book. Halfway through writing it in the first person, I had my major failure of nerve, and I switched to third. Maybe I was terrified to identify myself so closely with a central character who commits what was then, and still is, a criminal act in the United Kingdom (although the only way I could write the book was to block all thought of the inevitable consequences if it was published); just as likely, I found the prospect of handling the scenes where Paul and Gary declare their love too daunting: I'd be writing about something I'd never experienced, and the event seemed too overwhelming for me to write about it convincingly in the first person.

I sent the copy to a literary typist in England, Gertrude Young, whose name I found in the *Writers' and Artists' Yearbook*. She charged me about £3 for a top copy plus one carbon; I had some money left over from my summer job, and wheedled the rest out of one of my sisters with all sorts of promises. I sent the original to Heinemann, who returned it with a printed rejection slip after five weeks, and the carbon to Stephen Aske, the first name listed in the literary agents section of the *Yearbook*. The book was read there by Julian Jebb, the only staff member of the small agency apart from the owner, A. S. Knight (Stephen Aske did not exist – it was a name invented from Knight's initials). Jebb persuaded Knight, who demurred because of the homosexual theme, to handle the book. When it was eventually published in England and America, not a word was changed from the typescript, and no suggestions for changes were made by either publisher. Which was just as well: I'd written down my fictional dream to the utmost of my ability, but that ability was limited. If I'd been asked to make chamges, add scenes or expand existing material, change emphases – I don't think I could even have attempted to make the changes.

Over the next five months Jebb sent *Aubade* to five or six publishers who refused it. Gollancz turned it down after five weeks because he felt it would hurt me to have such a book published at my age. Katherine Whitehorn read it for Chatto and Windus, and later confided to readers of her *Observer* column that when she worked as a publisher's reader she was always having to read sensitive first novels whose hero was called Paul. Jebb kept faith in the novel. I lived for his letters, execrably typed with the mistakes x'd out or overtyped. He was my lifeline to the only future I could see for myself. I so badly wanted *Aubade* to be published I was afraid to think about what might happen to me if it was never accepted. While I waited, I spent the winter of 1956-57 learning shorthand and typing because everyone said a journalist had to know shorthand; though when I finally started working in Fleet Street I met no one else who took shorthand notes, and writers who shared offices with me complained that my typing sounded like a machine gun. But all my applications for trainee newspaper jobs in Northern Ireland were turned down, and I had no means of raising the money to move and establish myself across the Irish Sea in the fabled city of London.

In the afternoon on April 1, 1957 one of my sisters answered a ring at the front door. I found her standing beside me, grinning from ear to ear, her eyes shining and amazed, one hand behind her back. I couldn't believe what I was starting to hope. She held out a telegram. "Chapman and Hall will publish Aubade. £100 advance. Letter follows. Many congratulations. Jebb."

Two weeks later the contract arrived in a long brown envelope, and two weeks after that a cheque for £90. A week later I sailed for Liverpool with my belongings in a new fibreboard trunk. We'd had rare hot spring sunshine during my last few days at home, and I spent them sitting on the toolshed in the back yard, hoping to acquire a Hollywood tan. My first morning in London in the Southampton Row hotel, I noticed that there were irreparable cracks in the tan. I stood in front of the bathroom mirror and pulled away thick strips of brown skin to reveal the fresh face of a boy who had no idea what he was getting into.

Yesterday I made myself read *Aubade* again in order to write this introduction. I'd been able to force myself to read it once before, over twenty years after I wrote it, in 1978 when I was 38 and had just graduated *summa cum laude* and *phi beta kappa*, and won the Pack Prize in Psychology, from Columbia University in New York City. It took that much achievement to buffer the pain and the bitter memories the book held for me. For much of my life I associated *Aubade* with so much hurt and confusion that I even refused to acknowledge that I'd written it. I remember a battle in the late 1960s with a writer on the *Daily Telegraph Magazine* who was assigned to write the biographical box under a feature I'd written. When she mentioned that she'd read one of my novels I heatedly prohibited her from mentioning that I'd ever written fiction. "It took me years to get accepted as a journalist because nobody took me seriously," I said, unaware of the illogical subtext of what I said. Of course I had all kinds of reasons for wanting to deny that I was the man who'd written *Aubade*. There was its assertion of the sexual identity I became willing to acknowledge only on selected occasions; there was my repudiation of the agonizing emotions and social blunders of a boy who'd been given more than he could handle and then watched it evaporate; there were bad memories of years when I'd almost starved in pursuit of a promise that had failed. And to read the book at any time in my life is like opening a time capsule, sealed in 1957, which contains an accurate forecast of the miseries I created for myself.

Yet *Aubade* seems magical to me now. The grown-up writer cringes at the snobbery, and at Paul's Darwinian heartlessness, rooted though they are in the terrible pain of adolescence. But much of the book is so dead-on, the writing perfectly matched to the subject matter – adolescence from the white-hot interior. I'd forgotten how much fun I got out of Bryan and Mrs McKenzie; and how attached I was to sea and landscape, which Paul imagines are all he'll remember in years to come of the summer he didn't understand himself. Not so, Paul. What you remember is the people, and they influence you forever.

What interests me now is how I changed my experience, either in an attempt to order and understand what was happening to me, or to fit it into the kind of novel I wanted to write. First came the denial that I was Irish, which accounts for the absence of local place names in the book and a general avoidance of pinning down even the country where the action was taking place. I was born in Belfast (in the Midnight Mission in Malone Place), and grew up in

Bangor, the seaside town twelve miles from Belfast. As a Northern Irish Presbyterian, raised in a postman's family where only one other child went to grammar school and where no one read books as an adult, my culture was the official culture, inculcated at school, in films and on the radio. That culture was almost entirely English and American. In the first form at my grammar school, Upper Sullivan in Holywood, the small town between Bangor and Belfast, we were handed a slim green history of Ireland but were never required to read it. Perhaps the education authorities felt such controversial material was best left to parents to teach. Since my parents were poorly educated and talked only about the immediate concerns of getting through the day, I grew up in an historical and ideological vacuum, not even knowing *why* we went to different schools from the Catholics, lived in different neighbourhoods and took it for granted we'd have as little to do with them as possible. The only Ulster writer I read at school was the poet Louis MacNeice; in sixth form English literature we concentrated on the writers who wrote in English and lived across the sea rather than the Catholic Irish writers who wrote in English – we studied T. S. Eliot rather than Yeats, *Lord Jim* rather than *Dubliners*. So in my first novel I automatically denied my inheritance. The dialogue is so formal partly because I spent weeks before I wrote the novel studying Fowler, and was far more interested in correct syntax than reproducing colloquial speech, which in the case of my family would have been full of Ulster idioms. In my experience such speech did not belong in literature.

I also cleaned up my sixteen years of living, partly to make them manageable in a story, partly because I was ashamed of where I came from. Paul lives in a yellow house by the sea outside town; I lived in a four-storey terrace house in Dufferin Avenue, where I climbed a hill past shops and the Labour Exchange to a pub and the railway station, and ran parallel to Railwayview Street, one of Bangor's real "Bullrings". Paul is a late only child, born after another child dies; I was adopted into my family to replace a child who died, born when the woman I thought was my mother was in her forties. I didn't learn I was adopted until long after I wrote *Aubade*, but it seems clear from the story that I sensed or had overheard that I was adopted. It wasn't hard to guess: I was much taller than anyone else in the family, and fair, whereas they were dark, and emotionally expressive, whereas they had learned to hide everything. (But I also closed down when I was eighteen or nineteen, for about twenty years.) Far from being an only child, I had two brothers and two sisters, already the age you'd have expected my parents to be when I was an infant. It was my sisters who raised me, although my supposed mother and I fought a long battle over my autonomy.

There is much talk in the book about shortage of money and the prospect of scrimping to send Paul to university, but no one goes hungry or short of pocket money. My family always ended up eating something, but there were many days when we faced the prospect of no dinner at all. (When I ordered Irish stew in England I expected to be served fried onions mixed into mashed potatoes with Bisto gravy.) The man I called my father retired as a postman when I was seven or eight; his monthly pension was about £5. One brother died of TB when I was nine; the other worked as a butcher and then part-time as a window-cleaner. Only one family member, my older sister, had a regular job as a typist. The other sister helped my mother with the boarders we relied on to pay the bills. But visitors to Bangor from England and Scotland grew scarce as Europe opened up again after the war and the package tours business began to thrive. The Anderson family in *Aubade* has space for privacy and decent clothes and an altogether middle-class idea of poverty. I remember an old red winter coat my demoralized sister wore year in, year out, and I remember a pair of shiny brown trousers I wore to school for a year when everyone else was wearing grey. That's not memory exaggerating adolescent embarrassment. At an annual prize-giving, I checked and saw that I was the only boy not wearing the regular grey trousers of our school uniform; instead of looking forward to going up to collect my English prize in front of everyone, I dreaded it. On the one or two occasions I saved a few shillings as I child it was purloined to buy food. So unlike Paul, going to Queen's University in Belfast was never a real option for me. I'd have had to go back to school for a year to pass more A-levels just to get in, and I knew my family couldn't bear the expense of books and clothes and supporting me for three more years. I remember when I was thirteen or fourteen hearing my mother and sister talk: "We shouldn't hide how hard things are from him." I wondered then if they really thought they'd sheltered me from the harshness of our lives, but now I wonder if indeed there was much worse I never learned about.

I wish we'd been proud of our ability to transcend our poverty, had enough education to use it as a springboard to act for change. But I think we were all ashamed: of belonging to a family where the men didn't earn, of being at high risk for the disease that caused my brother to cough his lungs out for two years in a prefabricated National Health hut in the back yard. I grew up afraid to breathe. I hated going to see my brother David because I loathed the thought of catching the disease far more than I cared for him. My sister who worked as a typist refused to be X-rayed. She didn't talk about her reasons, but I'm sure it was because she was afraid she was infected and would be kept away from work and stop earning. Eight years ago, nearly forty years after I was exposed to TB, I had to take a skin test at the hospital where I was doing a clinical psychology internship. I still carried the TB antibodies. I remember my joy when I saw the red welt on my arm: I'd begun to enjoy living in a world that forced me to be authentic, to carry the markers of who I really was.

I replaced my father in my mother's bed, and slept with her until the night I told her she smelled. From as early as I can remember, my father and brothers slept in two beds in the unheated whitewashed coal shed in the back yard, the cement floor by their beds covered with candle grease and butts and ash from the Woodbine cigarettes they smoked in bed at night. My father handed my mother his pension once a month, and occasionally she'd ask him what he wanted to eat if my sister didn't ask him first. (Almost everything we ate came out of the frying pan, eggs and bacon and soda bread fried in lard.) Otherwise I don't recall my parents speaking to each other throughout the sixteen years I lived in their house. Mr and Mrs Anderson in *Aubade* are at war, but they fight out in the open. We had uncles and aunts and cousins in Bangor but no one came to visit, perhaps because we carried the TB stigma or because we were the poorest branch of the family. I know we were too proud to ask for help; I also know that on the one or two occasions desperation forced us to ask, we were refused. None of my brothers and sisters had dates or friends. We were never sure when we'd have the money to go anywhere, but I know that's an unsatisfactory explanation. Other poor people went places.

To try and explain what went on in my family is like reconstructing the inner working of an extinct society that was mute and illiterate: our past was not mentioned, relationships were not explored. I make guesses from memories of gestures and the charged air and rare sudden tears. Everyone in the house was dominated by the mother, who worked till she dropped but only felt safe in her own house, as if she didn't really believe her attempts to achieve respectability could succeed. The women controlled the men in our house because they controlled what money we had. The sister who worked resented her mother's favourite, the one who stayed at home. The surviving brother went out in the evenings and drank himself stupid when he could afford to, standing alone at the end of the bar smiling to himself.

A few days after my brother died of TB my mother turned on me in a rage: "You've been allowed to run wild while David was sick. I'm going to put a stop to that." I thought: "She wishes I'd died instead of David." I think I stopped taking her seriously when she found accumulated deposits of semen on my bedclothes and tried to make me ashamed of masturbating, although she could not name aloud the activity she was blaming me for or explain what was so pernicious about it.

Depicting the emotional complexity of such a family was beyond the skills of a sixteen-year-old writer. In *Aubade* I wrote only about the bits I thought I understood, and I was striving for a conventional understanding. People didn't write books about families like mine. But the book is full of the tension of growing up in that house and my struggle to disengage. Much is almost reportage. You'd have recognized the real life counterparts of Mrs McKenzie and Bryan immediately, although I also elevated them to a more secure middle-class position. The real Mrs McKenzie was even more fun: she warred openly with her neglected husband, doted on her youngest daughter (her two daughters are also absent from the fictional family) and engaged in thinly-disguised competiton with my mother over the merits of their respective children. In the book Bryan leaves home and Paul stays. In real life I was already living in London when Bryan left home to join the RAF. One day in a London pub we finally revealed the details of each other's adoptions. He was killed in his early twenties in a canoeing accident on the River Trent.

Mr Swallow is also lifted straight from life, although the real-life character was married with grandchildren. I guess that wasn't interesting enough for my purposes as an author. I worked for him for three summers, and for the last two methodically stole money from the till. He knew I was doing it but could never catch me. I remember hesitating over including the thieving in the book. In the end I was willing to risk people thinking I was a queer, but not a thief.

Chapman and Hall had been Charles Dickens' publishers, and when I started exploring London I could imagine Dickens purposefully walking the streets of the Temple near his publishers' office in Essex Street, on sharp winter mornings when the air near the river smelled as if something was burning. In the 1950s the firm made most of their money from technical books, and their only major author was Evelyn Waugh. My publisher, Jack McDougall, had been at Oxford with Waugh, and I think paid his keep in the firm as long as he kept Waugh happy. He told me he sent Waugh *Aubade* in the hope of getting a quote, but Waugh disliked the book because of its subject matter. Which was inconsistent, McDougall said, considering some of Waugh's adventures at Oxford.

McDougall was tall and greying and impeccably courteous. He talked like a superbly educated upper-class Englishman except for lapses into slang which shocked a linguistic purist like me. He treated me as an adult and an equal, and listened attentively as I spouted about my Art and mispronounced words like "indictment". I think McDougall did take me seriously: he'd taken on *Aubade* because of the writing rather then the subject matter. He encouraged me to make up to homosexual writers for the sake of the book, and took me to a literary dinner where I met several of them, but he told me it would be a pity if I became part of the crowd. Each evening McDougall took the train to his American wife and three daughters in Gloucestershire and spent the evening drinking wine and reading Latin poetry. I suspect he regarded homosexuality as ideally a diversion of early manhood.

I expected Julian Jebb to be dark, because he signed his name in black ink, and tall and solid. I hoped we would fall in love at first sight and spend the rest of our lives together. But Julian was short and blond and cheerful and mannered and social-climbing; he was a descendant of Hilaire Belloc, and I even saw a picture of him in the *Tatler* sharing a joke with some frumpy girl in a shiny dress. No author ever received more attention from an agent than I received from Julian, who received little money and less gratitude in return. I couldn't prevent him seeing my weakness, and I had to take revenge on him for knowing me too well. He invited me to his basement flat in Edwardes Square for drinks with his friends and the closer I got to his front door the more the cells in my body hummed with nerves; the nearest I ever got to that feeling was when I was on acid, injected by a psychiatrist or given me by a friend. It would have been an anomaly if a seventeen-year-old from Ulster had been able to hold his own in the rather rarified social discourse that Julian and his friends from Cambridge were rehearsing.

I can't have been much fun for Julian even when we were alone. I was relentlessly cynical, which I now regard as a sign of deprivation. But I wanted to make entrances and be the brilliant centre of attention. Instead I blushed and stammered. On one occasion, when Julian invited me to meet Rosamund Lehmann, I walked through the door, shook her hand, sat down, felt dreadfully conspicuous and ill-at-ease, and fainted. "Poor boy," Rosamund Lehmann was saying, patting my hand as I came to. "Haven't you eaten today?"

Next morning I got up and went to work at whatever temporary agency office job I was doing that week for about £7 pay. I'd spent my £90 on moving to London, buying a grey suit (to wear at literary parties) at the Savoy Tailors Guild, and living without working for two weeks. I don't know how I learned that no social shame is final, that what people say is not necessarily so, that it's worth keeping going to see what you do next. In my late teens and early twenties, growing up among a foreign race I didn't recognise as foreign, I had a secret peer, a young Irish actress called Constance Smith. She'd had several movie roles, including co-starring with Tyrone Power in a movie made in England, but she hit the headlines when she was brought to trial for stabbing her film producer lover. The newspapers disclosed that she belonged to a large Irish Catholic family, at least one of whom had died of TB. When I read the story I knew that I was doomed to self-destruct in ways I couldn't even guess at: no one like me could ever get as far as I wanted to go. Yet I proceeded to fight the inevitable and somehow laid the basis for a future career. Although I still flushed and stammered I could get through one-on-one encounters and even meetings with two or three people, particularly if alcohol was served to calm my nerves and loosen my tongue.

Shortly after I arrived in London the twice-weekly tabloid *Reveille* revamped its midweek edition and emerged as *Fling*, aimed at the teenage market advertisers were discovering. I wrote a sample column and sent it to the editors, and four days later a half-page in *Fling* entitled *Meet Ken Martin* appeared with a picture of me, my teeth straightened and my acne scars removed. The copy included a sweet message to Christine Truman, a young tennis player who never quite managed to cut it, and a dressing down of some official who'd criticized teenagers. Which about exhausted my repertoire of topics for journalism. I wrote a weak second column which never appeared – the editor told me I was too young for *Fling*'s target market. To fulfil my six-week contract I walked the streets of Stepney searching for prostitutes to interview for an expose, and tried to write a piece on the sex lives of famous composers. "Chopin was a *homosexual*," someone in an office where I was working whispered to me. Then *Fling* folded a few weeks after it started: it had been as desperate for circulation and advertisers as I was for ideas. I was paid £90 for my contract and bought a pair of shoes and a coat for the winter and got ripped off for a haircut in the lower Tottenham Court Road.

Meanwhile the press hoopla had started. I loved every minute of it: I was the centre of attention, *expected* to talk about nothing but myself. L.A.G. Strong, who'd read *Aubade* for Chapman and Hall and supplied the quote for the dustjacket, also wrote the *People* crossword, and he tipped off the newsdesk that there was a shocking prodigy in town. I was interviewed by a furtive young reporter in a raincoat, and photographed slurping whiskey in a Fleet Street pub while I pretended to read Thomas Wolfe. True to character, I sought revenge on the small town which I perceived as rejecting me: "Bangor is a nice place," I told the reporter, "but socially and intellectually it's a slum." I was reported verbatim under the heading "Shy Boy, 17, Writes Novel That Will Shock". "Don't worry," the reporter said, "people forget what's in the paper three days later." In which case, what was the point of using him to publicize my novel? But he was wrong: the *Belfast Telegraph* never forgave me, and panned everything I ever wrote.

Olga Franklin interviewed me for the more upscale *Daily Mail*, also in a Fleet Street pub, but since I was under eighteen she reported that our drinking took place in a hotel. Journalists who interviewed me were in a quandary: they could mention the scandalous plot of *Aubade* in passing, but couldn't discuss it, because mention of homosexuality in the popular press was limited to moralistic denunciations or shocking revelations about the upper classes corrupting their inferiors. Franklin was visibly desperate for a peg to hang her interview on, and I was happy to help her. I told her I had a split personality: part of me was Kenneth, the serious, studious type, and part of me was Jamie, who was out rocking and rolling all night long. I was sharp enough to watch the mixed emotions playing across Franklin's face: relief at finding her angle, and a conviction that I was lying through my teeth. She made a weak stab at journalistic integrity: "Is this true?" she asked. The interview got a full page, with a trick photograph of me wearing glasses and dressed as serious Kenneth watching Jamie dance.

There were radio interviews and a TV appearance talking about the meaning of love with Jeanne Heal, a TV personality known for her humourlessness. The *Radio Times* ducked the plot of *Aubade* by calling me 'a teenage angry young man who has written a powerful novel'. In the hospitality room two of the production staff stood beside me and talked about me as if I wasn't there. "He's not what you'd expect," one of them said. Heal introduced me by saying my book was the kind she'd hide in a brown paper cover. "I don't think there is such a thing as love," I told the viewers. "Love is two people holding on to each other because they're afraid of being alone." Next day the TV critic of the *Evening Standard* remarked that considering the theme of my book, Jeanne Heal perhaps had more of a sense of humour than she was given credit for in asking me about love. Which was a nice cheap shot, but what did it mean? That homosexuals couldn't possibly know anything about love?

Freddie Young, a *Punch* editor, took me under his wing, coaxed two funny articles and some book reviews out of me, and introduced me to the homosexual literary world of London: Patrick Kinross, Paul Dehn, Terence Rattigan, Angus Wilson. Primed with gin and tonic and coming on to anybody who took an interest in me, I managed to survive large parties without fainting or being totally tongue-tied. But in addition to being shy I was green and brash. An MP made a pass at me at a party, but was put off by my naivety: he told me he was married and had children, so I had trouble understanding that he was queer. It took years for me to understand that the men who seemed so worldly to me had to fight to create self-respect as homosexuals, and they paid a price. "I like queers," a homosexual editor told me, "but they have far too much power."

I made no long-term friends. Angus Wilson invited me to dinner at Dolphin Square with his boyfriend Tony Garrett, a probation officer who later lost his job because of his association with Wilson. "Do you support the Establishment?" Wilson breathed at me over dinner, his breath smelling of warm sardines. He offered to give my publisher a quote, and when I phoned to thank him he told me he'd intended it to read "A very good first novel". But the publicity director at Chapman and Hall probed for more: "Do you think its moving? What about the style?" Which explains the odd syntax in the quote they eventually agreed upon: "A very good first novel written with fine economy, intelligent and extremely moving." Six months later Wilson turned his back on me at a party. I can only guess it was because I was clearly besotted with his boyfriend.

Other encounters with leading literary figures were rendered stillborn by my shyness and pride. After McDougall sent him an advance copy, Edward Sackville-West wrote me a fan letter that included the phrases we eventually used in the advertisements:

"*Aubade* is a real achievement. I shall re-read it – a thing one only does with works of art." He mentioned that Benjamin Britten had also read the book and sent an admiring message. I called Freddie Young to tell him about the letter. "Edward Sackville-West's house is the headquarters of the only surviving coven of witches in the country," Freddie told me. I had no means of knowing that he was being catty about the members of Sackville-West's household. I replied to the letter, asking if we could use the quote, and added: "I'm told your house is the headquarters of the only surviving coven of witches in England." I don't know how Sackville-West really interpreted the remark, but he wrote back to say that as far as he was aware I'd been misinformed. Julian Jebb met him at a party shortly afterwards and invited us both for drinks. I turned down the invitation, claiming another engagement: I was still angry with Julian for witnessing my social nervousness, and I didn't want a repeat performance.

The offical publication date of *Aubade* was October 21, 1957, the day after my eighteenth birthday. A week earlier Freddie Young wrote to say that I was summmoned to tea at the Dorchester with Somerset Maugham on the preceding Sunday. I excused myself, explaining that some friends were giving me a small birthday party. I almost persuaded myself that I refused because I didn't want anyone to know I was spending my birthday alone; in fact I was overcome with nerves at even the thought of meeting anyone so famous. Later Freddie told me Maugham said only that he thought *Aubade* was a very good book for someone of my age to have written.

When *Aubade* was published I was almost starving. I cleared about £6 in my weekly paycheck and the rent for my Goldhurst Terrace bedsitter was £4.4s.0d a week. The big event of the week was a full plate of food on Friday night at a fast service grill in Leicester Square, and afterwards the balcony at the latest CinemaScope film at the Carlton in the Haymarket. By Monday I was back to surviving on a hard roll and coffee for lunch – and dinner was slices of bread, with the scrapings from a jar of jam, from a loaf that was getting mouldy by Tuesday. I made my poverty worse by exhibiting the same perverse pride I'd learned from my family. L.A.G. Strong had nominated me for membership in PEN. After I accepted, the bills for the £2.2s.0d membership dues started arriving. To admit that I couldn't afford the dues was unthinkably shameful; instead I wrote a letter to the PEN president, David Carver, saying I didn't agree with the organizations aims and must therefore cancel my membership.

"You have a reputation for being an extraordinarily temperamental and difficult young man," a writer told me years later.

In these circumstances it was easy for me to miss the impact *Aubade* had on so many people; the reviews were far from uniformly good. The *Observer* and the *Listener* ignored the book. Penelope Mortimer panned it in the *Sunday Times*, writing that to say Kenneth Martin was promising was like saying an egg is promising, because it depends on how they both turn out. She managed to misquote a four-word phrase from the book ("When it was over" became "When it was all over") to demonstrate that I wrote cliches. Pamela Hansford Johnson's grudging review in the *New Statesman* said I'd made the same mistake Proust made in writing about homosexual relationships: I made them superior to any other kind. (Hansford Johnson brought up Proust on every possible occasion, as if the claim to have read him conferred automatic superiority.)

Then John Betjeman's review appeared in the *Daily Telegraph*: "Not many books by anyone so young are worth publishing, but this was." And one day I came home from work and opened the little twice-weekly green packet of press-clippings from Durrants (another bill I never paid) and found Elizabeth Bowen's review in the *Tatler*: "Resolves the mixed and complex emotions of adolescence into the timeless purity of art. Most books about such years come from the pressure of emotional memory: Kenneth Martin writes from the very heart of them." That Saturday I went down to Essex Street and walked by the Chapman and Hall offices, hoping to see the bustle of activity as they ordered extra printings of my book to meet the unprecedented demand. If there had been anyone there, I'd have died rather than confess my expectations. *Aubade* did go into a second impression and eventually sold about 5,000 copies – not bad for a book with a title most people didn't understand or know how to pronounce. Of course it wasn't good enough for me. I wanted film rights and serialization. If I could, I'd have written *Peyton Place*. I didn't understand that a book's sales are usually limited to the audience which is ready to hear what it has to say. The world at large didn't want to hear the message in *Aubade*.

What reviews like Betjeman's and Bowen's gave to me was the conviction I'd written something fine, even when I became bitter because I couldn't repeat the success, even when I tried to disown what I'd written because I wanted to become someone else. Sackville-West's letter had included the hope that I was already halfway through another novel; McDougall was also eager for another book. A £100 advance seemed like a lot of money when I was hungry. I wrote two more novels which reeked of promise but which I knew were not honest or deep. Julian Jebb inherited money and went abroad. I moved to the A.D. Peters Agency, and Peters gave me the attention which the money I earned for him deserved. I met him once. There were no more newspaper or TV interviews: most of the sensational publicity had little to do with what I wrote; I got it because I wrote anything at all at my age. By the time I was twenty I'd determined to put my dreams away and get real. I managed a little high-class whoring because of who I was, with men who cared for me and whom I cared little for, but I failed at selling myself in Piccadilly – I hadn't a clue about going about it successfully. I'd always tried to do some journalism, and by the late 1960s I was finally making a good living writing for the newspaper colour magazines. For I while I believed absolutely in what I was doing. When I stopped writing even journalism and moved to America, I trained as a clinical research psychologist, which meant writing prose that by definition was unintelligible to the average reader.

It seems inevitable to me now: for the kind of naturalistic writing I do I needed a depth of experience and an education; it was unrealistic to expect me to write more books as good as *Aubade* when I was eighteen. But by the time I was twenty I felt I'd disappointed everyone. I had a sad little lunch with Jack McDougall in the mid-60s, the first time I'd seen him in years. "You survived," he said. "Why wouldn't I?" I asked. He said: "A lot of my friends went under." I thought: I'm a phenomenon to you, to be observed and commented on.

I know one of the reasons I survived: the most salient thing about me, even more important than the imperative to be a writer, was that I was attracted to other men. Against all evidence, I learned to trust my own feelings and my own judgement, even as they led me through multiple disasters. Waywardly, sometimes ashamedly, I chose to be who I was.

Shortly after I moved to America in 1970 I lived for two years with my lover Dick Oliver, briefly in California and then in New York City. We split up with a lot of things unsaid, good and bad. We continued to stay in touch while I was in graduate school in Minnesota, but I never told Dick I was moving to San Francisco. He was an architect who'd become a curator of a New York museum, and about the beginning of 1986 I stopped hearing about him – he hadn't written the books he intended to write, and the interviews he loved to give about his latest exhibitions stopped appearing. I started figuring possibilities, and didn't like my conclusions. Just before Christmas 1987 I called the museum and was shunted from one employee to another until a woman told me bluntly that Dick had died of AIDS two years ago. I still ruminate over chances lost: I know Dick would have wanted to see me, I know he must have tried to find me when he got sick. It was a long time before I began to search for comfort. I'd spent 1983 and 1984 caring for AIDS patients, the last year as a counsellor at the AIDS clinic in San Francisco. I thought: If I made a difference to just one man (and it was hard for me to believe I'd done any good), then maybe Dick had someone who made a difference for him as he was dying.

Now I remember that over thirty years ago, an ordinary boy wrote a short novel about the kind of love he was impelled to seek, and men and women who shared the dream read it and knew they were not alone.

San Francisco, June 1988

PART ONE

CHAPTER I

I

PAUL first saw Gary at church. He sat in the pew in front, sometimes with a woman who Paul supposed was his mother, more often by himself. When Paul was bored by the sermons, he examined the back of Gary's head carefully. He always looked extremely clean. He had fair, dry hair, which stood up at the back, and little flecks of dandruff rested on the collar of his worn but well-cut grey suit. His skin was very clear, and light gold in colour. His cheeks were pale, and rather thin. If Paul leaned slightly to the side during a prayer, he could see that Gary's eyes were open. "He must be an atheist," thought Paul, and in those days he longed to convert him to Christianity.

But they never spoke to each other. One day they passed each other in the street, and when their eyes met, Paul said, "Hello," quietly and nervously. Gary seemed to look straight through him, and he gave no sign of recognition. Paul flushed, and looked away.

Paul did not know Gary's real name, so he called him Gary because that seemed to suit him. He had the clean-cut face of an American boy, although he seemed to be more sensitive than the typical campus hero. He had a brooding look, and he slouched when he walked. But his face was proud.

II

When Paul left school for good, summer was just beginning, and the days were long and hot. Paul spent them fidgeting in the garden, but from the beginning he was restless and nervous. In other years he had not felt lonely. He used to pass his summer days climbing over the rocks, and leaping daringly out to sea. Other people did not exist; the world was peaceful and beautiful; the summers ended too soon. When he was small, Paul acted everything that he did. When he was walking along the coast he would say "Shoot," and he imagined the cameras turning on a boy walking by the sea.

Those were the peaceful scenes of his early childhood, but there was a place where Paul went often, and it terrified him. It was a deep inlet far from where Paul lived. Shadowed by trees, the dark waters rushed down to the sea. There was a smooth rock which stood above the inlet, and there was a tree from which Paul could jump on to the rock. He would stretch himself down flat and look over the edge, to where the water swirled, foaming and sucking. Laboriously, he would bring large stones up to the rock, and when he had enough he pushed them all over the edge. They splashed into the water, but Paul could never hear them hitting the bottom. He sang thunderous, jarring music until the noise subsided. But the excitement did not last long enough, and soon he went to gather more stones. He was proud that he could lie on the smooth rock above the inlet, for it was dangerous. If he had slipped, he would have been killed, and usually he was a frightened child.

The place where Paul lived when he was young was very beautiful. His home was a yellow house by the sea, and from his room he watched the sea, for it changed with the seasons, just like the sky and the trees. There was another coast on the horizon, but when he was very young Paul did not know what it was. At times it was misty and unreal, and looked like a strangely-shaped cloud-mass. Behind the house where Paul lived with his parents there was a glen and a great pool which was fed by a white waterfall. In the distance, there were the houses that marked the boundary of the town.

A change came over Paul when he left school. The heat was suffocating, yet he did not swim during the daytime, as he had done in cooler summers. He was now frightened of meeting anyone on the beach. He wanted to be alone, yet he disliked other people seeing him when he was alone. The bathers came from the town in pairs, or larger groups, and they made Paul feel conspicuous and awkward. A scout troop had camped in the glen, and Paul was frightened to go into it, in case he met any of the older boys. When he saw them, he suddenly became very shy, and he flushed, and imagined that they were laughing at him.

So he confined himself to the garden, and lay in the sun and read books. None of them interested him very much, and he had to read several at a time, reading a few pages of one, then going on to another. At night, he listened to record programmes on the wireless, and he also began to smoke cigarettes. The first few made him sweat, so that he had to lean his head on a cold pillow, and keep moving it to make it remain cold. But presently when he smoked he intended to be sick, for he liked the feeling, and he drank lemonade out of a glass, and pretended that it was beer.

One afternoon, when Paul had been lying in the garden since early morning, and he could bear the heat no longer, he went into the kitchen, where his mother was baking. The oven was on, yet Mrs. Anderson did not seem to notice the heat. Paul's clothes were sticking to him, but he would not take them off, for he hated either of his parents to see his body. For a while he watched his mother's red fingers kneading the dough. She did it very capably and purposefully.

Paul said, "I'm thinking of taking a job for July and August."

Mrs. Anderson continued with her work: she seldom expressed her emotions. "Where will you get one?" she asked finally, as if that had probably not occurred to Paul.

"There was an advertisement in the paper for someone to serve in a tobacconist's shop in the town," said Paul.

"It would mean that you'd have to travel there every day," said Mrs. Anderson.

"Didn't I have to do that when I was going to school?"

"How much pay would you get?"

"Probably about two pounds ten a week."

Mrs. Anderson looked almost cheerful. "You could use it for pocket-money when you're at university," she said.

Paul sighed. His mother had planned his entire future for him. He was going to take a degree, and then he was going to teach.

"You don't still want to be an actor, do you, Paul?"

"No," Paul replied, knowing that it would be useless to argue. Actors were not respectable, they never knew for certain when they were next going to eat, they were immoral. Whatever else Paul might be, his mother would never allow him to be an actor.

After a moment's hesitation, Paul ventured, "But, Mother, do I have to go to university? I could perhaps get a job on a newspaper, or something. You know that I'm not suited to teaching, or anything academic."

"Of course you are," said Mrs. Anderson. "You're very good at French."

"I'm not," said Paul, "I'm just quite good. I could never get an honours degree in modern languages. I certainly won't get a scholarship on the results of this examination. I'll be lucky if I pass it."

"Of course you'll pass your examination, and it's very likely that you'll get your scholarship." She paused. "Otherwise, you know that it will be hard to send you to university . . . but you'll go, all the same."

Paul turned away. As he was going upstairs, Mrs. Anderson called, "Paul!"

He went back into the kitchen, and, lowering her voice, his mother asked, "What's your father doing?"

"Nothing," Paul answered. "All he ever does is hang around and get in the way."

It was true. Mr. Anderson had no friends and few acquaintances. He had not even any neighbours.

On a hot day, Paul too found the loneliness and the silence depressing.

"Why can't we live in the town?" he asked.

"You know we can't afford it, Paul," his mother replied. "This house is the only thing we own, and if we sold it we wouldn't get half its value."

Lack of money was the most promising obstacle to Paul's going to university.

"How can you afford to send me to university when all we've got to live on is father's pension?" Paul asked.

"I have a little money of my own, that I've kept for years," Mrs. Anderson replied.

Paul had often wondered if his mother had a private income. She came from a good farming family, but she had made a poor marriage. Her parents must have given her money before they disowned her. They had died years ago, and they had left her nothing.

Mrs. Anderson continued, "We can live on your father's pension, and my money will send you to university."

Paul tried to think of a good reason why he should find a job immediately. He rebelled against the thought of another four years of the grind that he had suffered at school. On winter evenings, watched approvingly by Mrs. Anderson, he had gone up to his room and tried to study. But he preferred books that were not on the examination course, and the set Shakespearian plays did not inspire him. Soon, he would pick up *Julius Cæsar*, one of his favourites, and begin acting the part of Mark Antony. He stood in front of the mirror, and played the part intensely, so that he sweated and trembled. He would promise himself that in just another five minutes he would begin studying again, but he continued to add on five minutes until he was incapable of doing any school work. All the time, his mother thought that he was studying, and when late at night he went down to the kitchen again, she would look at him approvingly.

Paul made a feeble resolution. "Mother," he said, "I don't want to go to university. I'm not suited to it, and I should only be miserable."

Mrs. Anderson rarely lost her temper, but now her eyes sparked and her lips grew thin.

"Listen, Paul," she said, "you're not going to be a failure like your father. I want people to see that I can give you a good education, and that you're clever enough to deserve it. Four years will pass quickly, and then you'll be able to get any job you desire."

"I want to get a job as soon as the examination results come out," Paul said stubbornly. "If I get a job on a newspaper and I train as a journalist for a few years, then I should earn as much money as if I were a teacher.

"If you get a job on a newspaper, you won't get enough money to keep yourself. And I won't keep you," shouted Mrs. Anderson. "You can get out of the house and go wherever you like. I don't get very much thanks, do I, for all the things I've given you?"

As she turned away, Paul saw the tears of anger in his mother's eyes. He felt sorry for her, but he did not regret hurting her. Paul realized that it was pride that made her want him to do well. She cared very little for him, yet she had brought him up, and managed to give him almost everything he wanted. Paul was her investment in the future, and if he left her, she would have nothing.

She had begun baking again. She was small, and her hands were the strongest part of her. Her mouth was set in a thin line, and her hair was shining white. She must have been pretty when she was young, for she had good features and her skin still glowed, although she was now old. Paul had worked it out that he must have been born when his mother was over forty; she was now almost sixty. There had been another child, but it died.

Paul said, "I'll go to university," and at once he felt an easing of the tension in the air.

Mrs. Anderson said, "It's about time you had some sense." She added softly: "Try and get a job for the summer, and you can use the money to buy books."

"I'll go and see the owner of the shop now," said Paul.

Then he went upstairs to his room, and lit a cigarette. If his mother had known that he smoked, she would have stopped giving him pocket money. He inhaled a few times, until he felt slightly sick, then he went over to the window and opened it. The sudden rush of air into the room was warm and sweet.

III

Paul decided to walk into the town, for his bike needed cleaning, and he was too lazy to attend to it. The sun was still shining brilliantly in the blue sky, and the coast road was dry and dusty. The rocks dropped away from it, down into the sea, and a green world which Paul loved to watch. The day was too hot for walking, and he was glad when he turned the bend in the road and came to the outskirts of the town.

The poorer inhabitants tried hard to turn the town into a sea-side resort, but the richer landlords tried just as hard to prevent them. Therefore the town had amusement arcades, dance-halls, and a swimming pool, but there was no pier pavilion, or any organized attempts at large tourist publicity campaigns. Nevertheless, the promenade was always crowded, and many young people had a good time. They intermingled more than their parents had ever done, and the upper-class girls had begun to dress in the fashion which had been reserved for shop-assistants and factory workers. It was one of the ways in which they could attract boys, if they were not inclined to go to church socials.

There were many, many badly attended churches in the town. The less well-known middle-class inhabitants of the town attended them constantly, but the richest inhabitants only visited them occasionally. The working class received no encouragement at all, and anyhow, most of them hated the sight of a church. Of course, there were also a few Christians in the town.

Paul soon discovered that the shop where he hoped to get a job was in Francis Street, one of the poorest districts in the town; it was nick-named "The Bullring". It was built on a hill, and the houses were tall and narrow. There were no front gardens; the doors opened on to the pavement. The drainage was bad. Paul shuddered to think what it would be like later in July, if the heat continued. He passed a newspaper shop, and a pub, and then found the shop, huddled between two houses. Across the road was a factory and a café. Above the door of the shop there was a sign, with "W. R. Swallow" printed on it. It was hard to make out, for the paint was peeling off. The window was shallow, and tobacco cartons for display had been arranged into some kind of pattern; they were dusty. Dead flies lay against the glass.

When Paul went into the shop, it was dark and he could not see: the light outside had been too bright. For a moment he stood, hearing the cries of the children in the street, and smelling the tobacco. Gradually he made out a man standing behind the counter, a man of medium height and fine build, with a lined face and a firm mouth.

"Good afternoon," he said distinctly, and bobbed his head and looked away. Paul flushed.

"I came in reply to your advertisement in the paper," he said formally. "It said that you wanted an assistant for July and August."

Mr. Swallow looked at the wall behind Paul's head, and began to scratch his neck gently. Paul suddenly wanted to start laughing. The pattern of

Mr. Swallow's blue suit reminded him of his own pyjamas.

Mr. Swallow twisted his face and asked, "Are you still at school?"

"I've just left," Paul replied.

Mr. Swallow opened his mouth to say something, then changed his mind. He kept his mouth open, and searched for something else to say.

"Where do you live?" he asked.

"About four miles round the coast," Paul replied, "but I have a bicycle of course. I could come to work on that."

Paul was a very bad business-man. He suddenly decided that he wanted to work for Mr. Swallow, no matter what the conditions of work were. He liked Mr. Swallow very much.

"What hours can you work?" asked Mr. Swallow.

"Whatever suits you," Paul replied.

"Well, the hours would probably be from ten in the morning to one o'clock, and from about half-past one to seven o'clock, with a break for tea, and Saturday and Sunday free." Mr. Swallow raised his voice at the end of the last sentence, as though he were asking a question.

"That's fine," said Paul. "How much pay will I get?"

"Two pounds ten?"

"Yes."

Paul realized that there had been no customers in the shop since he began talking to Mr. Swallow.

"Have you much business?" he asked.

"A fair amount," Mr. Swallow replied. "I'm busy in the evenings, especially on Friday, but in the afternoons I'm always slack."

Paul gazed round the shop. It was badly stocked, and the display of tobacco on the shelves was poor. There were a few half-empty jars of cheap sweets, with the lids only half-screwed on, and the labels turned towards the wall. Mr. Swallow did not seem to care very much about his shop.

There was a silence. Paul wondered why Mr. Swallow left him to take the initiative. Finally he asked, "Do you think I'll be suitable?"

"Yes," Mr. Swallow replied. "When can you start?"

"Any time," said Paul.

Mr. Swallow consulted a calendar. "If you start tomorrow, you'll have three full weeks before the end of the month." (Again he made the statement seem like a question.)

"All right," said Paul, "I'll come in at ten in the morning."

He backed out of the shop. As he pushed his way past the frowsy women standing in the doorways he breathed a sigh of relief. He hated being forced to make conversation with someone. To avoid the crowds of people on the promenade he cut down a side-street and headed towards the library.

IV

There was a large stock of books, but Paul could never find one that he really wanted to read. Anyhow, most of the serious books were too dull to read on a hot summer day. Paul had given in to his better judgment and chosen a beginners' book of philosophy when he heard someone say "Hello". He turned round and saw Robin Forrest, a boy who had gone to school with him. Robin looked genuinely pleased to see him. During the past year they had gone to a dancing class and a few pictures together, and they were on quite good terms, although they had never become really friendly. Robin was very popular at school: he played sports well, and still managed to do well in the classroom, while Paul tended to hover alone on the edge of the different cliques. He was half-admired, half-ridiculed.

"I didn't see you after the examinations," said Robin. "How did you get on?"

Paul hesitated. "Quite well in some subjects, and very badly in others," he replied. "What about you?"

"I think I did quite well," said Robin. "What you been doing with yourself? I haven't seen you around lately."

"I've been swimming, and lying in the sun," Paul replied. "To-morrow I start a job in a tobacconist's shop in the Bullring."

"That's a pretty tough district," said Robin.

Paul smiled. "I expect I'll survive."

They began to look at the books on the shelves, and Paul searched for something to say. "Are you going to university, Robin?" he asked.

"Yes, you are too, aren't you?"

Paul nodded. "It's a pity we won't be doing the same subjects," he said.

"Well, we can always travel up on the train together," said Paul. Again they were at a loss for something to say. Paul hurriedly chose another book, and said, "I'll go now, Robin. I have enough books."

"So have I," said Robin. "I'll come with you."

Paul was glad to have someone with whom to walk through the town, and on the way he tried to make light conversation about acquaintances and school activities, but they were still awkward with each other, and Paul knew that it was his fault. He was no longer interested in Robin, or similar people.

Robin insisted on walking all the way round the coast to Paul's home, and when Paul finally convinced him that there was no need for him to come any further, he said, "We'll have to go for a swim or a game of tennis sometime, Paul."

"I'd like to," Paul lied. When he saw that Robin wanted to fix a time there and then, he added hastily, "I'll ring you up—soon."

Robin hesitated, puzzled, but at last he said good-bye. Paul breathed a sigh of relief. He hoped that it was the last he would see of Robin for a long time.

CHAPTER II

I

Mr. Anderson was sitting in the kitchen. Paul went into the scullery and said to his mother, "I've got the job. I hope you don't mind my working in the Bullring."

"It can't be helped," said Mrs. Anderson. "How much pay are you getting?"

"Two pounds ten a week."

"Good," said Mrs. Anderson. "Paul, Mrs. McKenzie rang up while you were gone. She's visiting us to-morrow night."

Paul flushed. "Is she bringing Bryan?" he asked.

"Yes," replied Mrs. Anderson. "Paul, I want you to promise me that you'll behave well with Bryan. I don't want any arguments. You know the way Mrs. McKenzie talks."

"Of course there won't be any arguments," said Paul coldly. "I only hope that Bryan behaves as well as I do."

"You can be sure that Mrs. McKenzie has given him his instructions," said Mrs. Anderson. "Are you going to go around with him this summer?"

"I don't know," Paul replied.

"Surely you can find nicer friends," said Mrs. Anderson.

"Of course I can," said Paul, "but what's the use —when I grow tired of them after so short a time. I met Robin Forrest to-day and he asked me to go out with him, but I don't like him any more. At least I like him, but I don't like being with him. If I go out with Bryan, we can soon have a good argument and end the thing decently."

"That's much too cynical a remark for a boy of your age," said Mrs. Anderson. "No wonder you have no friends nowadays."

"I have no friends because I don't want any," said Paul sharply.

"Everyone wants friends, even if they do pretend otherwise," said Mrs. Anderson.

"You can't understand," said Paul. "Up to now I've always been glad of company and I've never been alone. But now I want to be alone. Robin and the rest of them are a lot of silly children. The only things they care about are playing games and going to the pictures and having girl-friends. It's as if each of them had been turned out of the same mould; they haven't had an original thought in their lives. Well I'm different, and I'm proud of it. I don't want to have to spend the rest of my life learning how to conform to a set of rules that a lot of foolish people have made. And I don't care about being a social success. And now that you're going to make me go to university, I'm not getting a degree just to please Mrs. McKenzie and Bryan; I want to learn something about life."

It was a pretentious speech, and Paul had read most of it in a magazine belonging to his mother. Mrs. Anderson gave no sign that she recognized it, however, and she seemed to take it seriously enough.

She said, "You're going to be an idealist, so you'll be very unpopular."

"That's an example of what I meant," said Paul. "You immediately thought of other people's reactions. Surely your own beliefs are as important to you as other people's."

"Of course they are," said Mrs. Anderson, "but you have to meet other people half-way, or you can't live, unless you want to be a hermit."

Paul said, "I think that with you other people are more important than yourself."

"Probably," said Mrs. Anderson.

"In that case," said Paul, "the world is all wrong."

Paul half-believed his own arguments, but he knew that he would never be brave enough to test them. He was much too conscious of other people ever to defy their beliefs. He would not have dared to try and discuss religion or philosophy with Robin

Forrest, for he knew that he would be ridiculed. And anyhow Robin's opinions had no interest for Paul. Books on philosophy and religion bored him, and when other people talked about those subjects, Paul believed that he had heard all their arguments before.

Perhaps he was neither strong enough nor weak enough : strong enough to go among other people and defy them, weak enough to let them mould his beliefs until they were insipid and pliable.

Paul carried a tray of food into the kitchen, and his mother followed him.

Mr. Anderson said, "Paul's so tall that soon he won't be able to get through that doorway."

Mrs. Anderson gave a tiny smile, but did not reply. After a moment Mr. Anderson looked down at the ground again. He was ugly : dressed in shabby trousers and a cardigan. It occurred to Paul to wonder how his father was going to spend the summer, but he decided that he was so old it did not really matter.

"Would either of you like a cup of tea?" Paul asked politely.

"Please," said Mrs. Anderson.

"Would you like one, Father?" asked Paul.

"Yes," said Mr. Anderson, raising his eyes from the floor.

Paul poured out the tea, and set three places at the table. Mr. Anderson pretended not to see.

"Your tea's out, Father," said Paul.

Mr. Anderson looked round. "Thank you, son," he said. His voice was hoarse from smoking too many cigarettes, and he also coughed frequently.

When his parents were seated at the table, Paul began eating. He had nothing to say, neither had Mrs. Anderson, but every action of her husband's seemed to annoy her.

Finally she said, "Harry, must you put sugar on your bread? There's plenty of jam."

Mr. Anderson looked at her with an expression of righteous anger. His eyes were yellow and bloodshot. He said, with an attempt at sarcasm, "I'm sorry. There was no jam yesterday."

Paul looked away in disgust. Did his father realize how childishly he was behaving, or did he believe that his reply was clever.

Mrs. Anderson looked at Paul despairingly, expecting him to sympathize with her. For a moment, Paul felt a strange pity for his father, and he stared at his mother coldly.

"Father, I'm going to take a job for July and August," he said.

"Thank you for telling me," said Mr. Anderson.

Paul felt despair, and the beginning of anger.

"What kind of reply is that to give to your own son?" asked Mrs. Anderson. "You should be ashamed of yourself. All you do is sit on your back-side all day and make bad-tempered remarks."

"I'll make whatever kind of remarks I want to," said Mr. Anderson. "I think I'm still master of my own house although there's no one who wants me."

Suddenly Paul hated his father.

"Why don't you get a job and give yourself something to do?" he asked him, "instead of hanging around getting in people's way."

That morning, in the garden, everything Mr. Anderson did seemed calculated to annoy Paul. Now he rose from his chair as if he were going to strike him.

"My, but you're a fine example of what education can do for a boy," he taunted. "You've got no manners, and you don't care a damn for anyone but yourself. If you don't shut your mouth, you'll get a job for good and start bringing money into the house like you should be doing."

"That's none of your business, Harry," Mrs. Anderson interrupted, with panic in her voice. "I'm paying for Paul's education. I haven't asked you for a penny."

"By Jesus it's my business," shouted Mr. Anderson. "He'll do whatever I tell him to do."

Paul knew that his father did not really believe that. He might rage, but he was weak, and each day he was becoming more incapable of positive action.

29

He shouted, "The way you two behave you'd think there was an agreement between you to annoy me." Paul was compelled to keep silent by his mother's look.

"Well, I won't stand for it," shouted Mr. Anderson. "From now on I'll be master in my own house, or you can both get out and stay out. You'll at least be civil to me. Do you hear me?"

Neither Paul nor his mother replied. At last, in a final spasm, Mr. Anderson shouted, "Christ, I won't stand for this. When I speak to you, you'll answer me or I'll knock your bloody faces into hell." He rushed out of the room. Paul could hear him coughing in the yard outside; at the end of each cough he struggled for breath before he began again; often he coughed just to annoy his wife or Paul, but this time it seemed genuine.

Mrs. Anderson was white-faced and shaken.

"Paul, I can't go on like this any longer," she said. "Harry gets more bad tempered every day, and there's no one whom I can ask for advice."

By now she had forgotten that the row had begun partly through her own fault, and Paul knew his mother never guessed that she was at all responsible for her husband's degradation.

"Why did you ever marry him, Mother?" Paul asked gently.

"I don't know, Paul."

"Was he always bad-tempered?"

"No," replied Mrs. Anderson. "When I first met him, he was too proud to lose his temper. That was one of the reasons why I was so attracted to him."

Paul saw that his mother seemed to take pleasure in recalling the times before she was married, and he encouraged her to tell him about them, hoping that she would grow calmer.

"Your father was different from all the other boys I knew," said Mrs. Anderson. "I used to have plenty in those days, but I was a headstrong girl, and though I was engaged several times, I always broke it off, I always broke it off before it was too late. I first noticed your father because he seemed independent of all girls. He used to go shooting and riding with two or three other boys, and he went to dances, but he rarely asked a girl to go out with him. Perhaps it was because he was so poor, for although his father was one of the most respected men in the town, he had no money. But poverty didn't prevent other boys from having fun.

"Everyone knew Harry Anderson was independent and proud. The others used to tease him about it, and tried to make him unbend a little. And often girls tried to flirt with him. It must have taken a great deal of courage for him to ask me out, for he knew how everyone would tease him when they saw him with a girl.

"One night, when I was coming home from a dance, my bicycle got a puncture, and your father took me home on the back of his motor-bike. When we came to my house, he asked me to come to the next dance with him, and he offered to collect my bike for me next day. I agreed, and from then on it was an accepted fact that we were going out together.

"It was springtime, and at the week-ends we went into the country, and roamed over the fields. At the beginning of the summer Harry asked me to marry him. I accepted, partly to spite my parents, who thought it was a poor match, and partly because all the other girls were jealous. We had a large wedding, and then my father gave me some money, and told me that I would never get any more.

"Harry's father gave him this house. It was his only possession, but we had nowhere else to go, so we had to leave home and all our friends and come and live here. Harry soon got a job, and at first we were rather happy. We went to dances and made some passing friendships. We didn't mind the loneliness.

"Then the years passed, and we had no children, and we grew lonely. We had never had very much in common, and now we began to fight and argue. At one time it seemed that I was going to have a child, but I lost it. Then you came, and for a while we were happy again. But when your father retired we had no money saved, and he got a very small pension. With nothing to do, he became more bad-tempered every day, and he was too proud to take another job. I vowed that you would never have that kind of problem. All these years I've kept the money my father gave me, so that you can have a good education and a good start in life.

"That's why you must go to university."

Paul had only guessed these things before. Now he realized how much his education meant to his mother. Her son was the only thing for which she had to live.

Paul said, "Then you have nothing to worry about, for I told you that I'd go to university."

Mrs. Anderson smiled. "Good," she said, "I'm depending on you."

Although Paul had just been told the details of his parents' life together, he realized that the knowledge made him no nearer to his mother. She could have told exactly the same story to a stranger, for she was completely unselfconscious.

Paul went upstairs to his room and, without switching the light on, looked out of the window. The beach was deserted. He decided to go for a swim.

Paul slipped off his sandals. The sand was still warm, and for a few moments he buried his feet in it. Below the top layer it was cold and damp.

The sun gradually approached the islands on the horizon. Paul had never been there, but he thought that they were uninhabited, with beaches and woods and birds.

The water was very cold, and at first he could hardly breathe. He swam out to sea quickly, a long way out. He was a good swimmer and he took pride in it, for otherwise he was unathletic. At last he lay on his back, and let the water lap gently round and over his body. From the shore the sea had appeared calm, but now he could feel and hear its motion, a roaring and sucking far below him.

The sky was still blue, but it was fading, before it grew darker again at night time. Looking at it made him dizzy, so he closed his eyes.

For a year now, Paul had been waiting : through the winter and the spring he had done things which he would never before have dreamt of doing. The restlessness had made him attempt long walks on damp, dark evenings. When he came home to the warmth of his room, he acted the most emotional scenes from the books he owned. He could not sit still to learn a piece of poetry: he walked about the room with the book in his hand. The only time he could be at peace was when he had a cigarette to smoke, and a love song was being played on the radio.

He swam farther out to sea, for he was growing cold.

The summer stretched before him, and still he did not know what he was waiting for. At least he saw that he must not be alone, but he could not help avoiding people. When he was with them he was sometimes happy, sometimes awkward, but afterwards he always dreaded being with them again. None of his friends had ever been very attractive, anyhow. There had never been anyone with whom he had desired a lasting friendship; at least, there had been a few, but he was too shy to approach them.

Except Bryan, but then his relationship with Paul could hardly be called friendship; it was more a friendly enmity. Each of them was very much aware of the other's faults.

Paul's eyes were suddenly hot. He closed his eyelids but it was too late. He was crying, in short hard sobs.

When he arrived back at the house it was night time. The lights of the town glowed behind the sky-line, and outshone the stars. His sandals made a queer sucking sound as he climbed the stairs, for his feet were still wet.

He switched on the light in his room. It was a pleasant room, large and well-furnished. Behind the wardrobe and the bed there was an empty space where he acted the plays. In the bookcase with five shelves there were some paper-backed books, but a good many expensive ones. Paul bought many of the books and never read them. He had read all the novels, and the books on acting technique and the stage, and all the plays, but the books of psychology and philosophy remained unopened. Much of the poetry was also unread, but sometimes Paul grew to love a lyric, and without any effort he knew it off by heart, because he had read it so many times.

Paul dried his body and his hair, then dressed slowly. He liked good clothes, for they gave him self-confidence. He put on a pair of slacks and a striped jersey, then lit a cigarette and sat down on the edge of the bed, to plan what he would do with his time. He would be working during the daytime. At night he could go to the pictures, or come straight home from work and go for a swim and read a book. If he planned carefully, he would always have something to do. But the thought of having to plan so carefully depressed him.

He found that he could bear the thought of being with Bryan, but he would have to see how Bryan behaved to-morrow night.

CHAPTER III

I

IT seemed that it really was going to be a beautiful summer. The next morning the sun was shining brightly again, and the sky was cloudless. In the Bullring the women were standing sunning themselves and gossiping with their neighbours, while the men hung around in dirty unbuttoned vests. As Paul walked up to the shop, he smelt the food from the café, mingled with the stink from the people and the drains.

Mr. Swallow was sitting alone at the back of the shop. He spent the first few minutes of the day teaching Paul the prices of the different brands of tobacco, and soon there was very little left for him to learn. Very few customers came into the shop, and there was a pathetically small amount of money in the till. Paul was allowed to do almost exactly as he wished. Mr. Swallow sat at the back of the shop checking accounts, and not interfering with him.

"Do you live near the shop?" asked Paul.

"In the house next door," replied Mr. Swallow.

Paul had noticed it as he came in. The plaster was broken from the walls, and above the door was a notice advertising a brand of cigarettes.

"Have you made any arrangements for having your lunch?" Mr. Swallow asked shyly.

"No," replied Paul. "I thought that I might have it in the café across the road."

"If you like," said Mr. Swallow, "I'll leave you some in my house, and when I come back each day, you can go in and eat it."

Paul thanked him. It would save money, and it would hardly inconvenience Mr. Swallow very much.

"Have you got a girl friend?" asked Mr. Swallow.

"No," replied Paul, "and I don't think I want one."

"Well," said Mr. Swallow, "if you do, there are some nice girls working in the factory across the road."

"They can't be worth much," said Paul, "if they work in a place like that."

"They aren't very intelligent," said Mr. Swallow, "but some of them are quite good-looking."

"Girls usually bore me," said Paul. "I used to go around with them quite a lot, but now I'm tired of them. Do they ever come over to the shop?"

"Just on pay-days," replied Mr. Swallow. "That's the only time when they have any money. They only get thirty shillings a week."

"That's terrible," said Paul. "Surely they could get a better job?"

"They have no ambition, unless it's to marry early and be forced to have a large family."

"And I expect their husbands are as badly paid as themselves," said Paul.

"Probably."

While Mr. Swallow was away for his lunch, one of the girls from the factory came into the shop for some sweets. She was dressed in the jacket of an old suit, and a pair of unglamorous jeans. She had adenoids, and a dripping nose, and Paul had often heard her type caricatured on radio shows. She made a great show of counting her money, which consisted of pennies and ha'pennies, and she bought an ounce of several different kinds of sweets, and had them put in separate bags. Altogether, she did not buy more than sixpenceworth.

She seemed inclined to talk.

"When do you get your holidays from the factory?" asked Paul.

"I'm not taking any," the girl replied. "We don't get paid when we take holidays."

"Nothing at all?" asked Paul incredulously.

"No," replied the girl. "Anyhow, I wouldn't have been going anywhere, so I might as well work." She shrugged, and dismissed the subject. Holidays were outside the scope of her ambitions.

"How many girls work in the factory?" asked Paul.

The girl counted on her fingers. "Seven, and one boy."

"What does he do?" asked Paul.

"Oh, he's only working there for the summer," said the girl. "He's a student or something. He supervises us to make sure that we work hard. Nobody ever talks to him very much."

"What's his name?" asked Paul, "I may know him."

"I don't know his first name," said the girl, "but his second is Knight," She giggled, and seemed to think that was a very funny name.

When Mr. Swallow returned, he handed Paul a key.

"Go in and have your lunch now," he said, "and when you come out, lock the front door." Paul thanked him and left the shop.

While he worked in the shop, he only saw the hall and the kitchen of Mr. Swallow's house, but they were incredibly dingy and shabby. Paul shuddered when he thought of what it would be like to live there.

His dinner had been left on the kitchen table. It consisted of two potatoes, a slice of fried bacon, and a pot of strong tea, with two slices of bread and margarine. While he ate the food, Paul examined the small, dark room. There was electric light, but there did not seem to be a radio. There were no books or magazines, and the few letters lying on the mantelpiece seemed to be bills or circulars. On the walls there were photographs, all of Mr. Swallow, standing or sitting alone. The first had been taken when he was a little boy, and the most recent was dated five years ago. In the room there was no indication that Mr. Swallow had any relatives, or even friends.

When he had finished his meal, Paul left the house, locking the door behind him. Back in the shop, as he handed the key to Mr. Swallow, he asked, "Are you sure it isn't too much trouble making me a meal at lunchtime?"

Mr. Swallow looked worried. "No, no," he said, staring at the floor. Then he retired to the back of the shop. Paul sat down behind the counter, and fiddled with the tobacco cartons. One thin beam of the bright sunlight had wedged itself between the roof of the factory across the road and the top of the shop window. It shone across the counter, making the dust glitter, and made a thin band of light on Paul's wrist. He watched the hairs shine, and felt the brown skin grow warm.

"One of the girls from the factory told me that there's a student working there," said Paul. "Do you know him?"

"Yes," replied Mr. Swallow, "he comes over here for cigarettes, and sometimes he stands and talks for a while. He's a medical student, but I think that now he's passed all his examinations. He must be working in the factory to pass the summer. He's a very nice lad."

"What age is he?" asked Paul.

"Twenty, or twenty-one."

The warm afternoon passed very slowly. Mr. Swallow seemed to be quite contented checking accounts, while Paul served the few customers. None of them was willing to talk for any length of time, and soon Paul felt bored and lonely.

"You don't do very much business, do you?" said Paul.

"It's just fair," said Mr. Swallow. Paul would have called it very poor, and he wondered why he had been engaged to work in the shop. Probably because Mr. Swallow grew very lonely by himself. Paul had noticed that one of the ways he occupied himself was by cutting out coloured figures from display cartons, and pasting them on the backs of the showcases. It seemed a childish occupation.

For a while Paul dusted and cleaned but then there was nothing else to do. He knew that he could not bear this idleness for the rest of the summer.

"May I bring a book with me to-morrow?" he he asked. "I get bored sitting here."

43

"Of course you can," replied Mr. Swallow, "you'll soon get used to the quietness."

It seemed unlikely.

Finally tea-time came and Mr. Swallow went into his house again. Paul wondered what he would have for tea. Probably bacon sandwiches.

Soon the workers in the factory finished. Paul watched them as they left. They were mostly like the girl who had come into the shop, although some of them wore better clothes. Last of all came the boy who Paul supposed was the medical student. When he left the factory, he went into the café next door. Paul had seen him before. He was the boy he called Gary, the boy who sat in front of him in church a long time ago.

Mr. Swallow returned in about ten minutes. "Where are you going for your tea?" he asked.

"The café across the road," replied Paul.

Gary was eating fish and chips at one of the tables. When he heard Paul come in, he looked up. Paul glanced away immediately, before their eyes met. He sat at a table just behind Gary, and he found himself examining him just as he had done in church two years ago.

He had not changed. His hair was still untidy, looking as if it had just been washed. His skin was still light golden, and to Paul he seemed very well dressed, although he was wearing a conventional

44

tweed sports coat, and his brown casual shoes needed heeling. He ate his food leisurely, and drank only a glass of milk. Paul ate his food quickly, and gulped down several cups of coffee. He finished just as Gary lit a cigarette. Immediately Paul was frightened that if Gary got up he would turn round and look at him. Paul could not understand his own fear, but he got up and left the café. He heard Gary behind him, just a few feet away, but he let the door swing back, so that Gary would have to open it again. Impulsively Paul went on down the road, and into the pub. Through the open doorway he saw Gary passing on down the road, with his eyes on the ground, and the slouch that Paul remembered.

Paul had never been in a pub before. He ordered a glass of cider, and as he lifted it, he was shocked to see that his hand was trembling. He could not understand the effect that Gary had on him. He had never experienced it before.

He took two bottles of beer back to the shop, and at first Mr. Swallow would hardly believe that they were for him. He tried to make Paul drink one of them, but Paul was frightened of the effect that it might have on him. He decided that soon he must buy a bottle of whisky and drink it in private.

"How can you afford to buy beer?" asked Mr. Swallow. "I thought you were saving up for a holiday on the Rivieria."

"Where?" asked Paul, smiling.

"The Rivieria," repeated Mr. Swallow.

"It's the Riviera," said Paul.

"No, it isn't," said Mr. Swallow crossly. He had an endearing faith in his own knowledge.

Paul wondered where Gary had been going when he left the café. Probably to the pictures, although it was rather early. He would hardly have arranged to meet anyone at that time. Paul was glad to imagine that Gary was going by himself. In the days when he had seen him at church, Paul had often watched him waiting in his car for a friend. Paul was jealous of them all. Gary was exactly the kind of friend he wanted, yet it was impossible. His car had been long and sleek, satin-white in colour, so he must be rich, and move in an entirely different circle of acquaintances from Paul. And he was years older, and he must be clever, for Mr. Swallow said that he had already passed all his examinations. Paul envied him. With a lovely car, and money to give him security, Paul too could have worked very hard, and been a success.

II

When he arrived home, Paul heard Mrs. McKenzie's voice in the kitchen. He decided to go upstairs to his room and dress. He felt a curious nervousness about meeting Bryan and Mrs. McKenzie. He knew that Bryan might adopt any attitude towards him, and Mrs. McKenzie would be critical, and occasionally unpleasant, in the most unobtrusive way.

He shaved and dressed carefully, taking longer than necessary. Then he smoked a cigarette, but he could still feel an emptiness in his stomach. Finally he picked up a short novel which was one of his favourites, and read the poem which was included in it. It was a translation from the Sanskrit, called "Black Marigolds," and Paul thought that it was probably the most beautiful poem ever written. It was weary with the sadness of a man who remembers his first love, the most beautiful of all. Yet Paul did not know why it appealed to him, for he had never been in love with anyone; he had never begun to love anyone.

III

Mrs. Anderson met Mrs. McKenzie on one of her infrequent visits to church. Paul's mother found many excuses for her own absence from church, although she vowed that there was not a single thing to prevent Paul from going. Mrs. McKenzie went regularly, and dragged her son with her.

They lived in one of the better-class districts of the town, and Mr. McKenzie, who always stayed in the background, occupied a highly paid position in the Civil Service. He had a number of friends, for he was an inoffensive person, but his wife was ignored by her own class, so her few friends were poorer and lived in less respectable districts. She was a kind woman, but she was invariably dressed shabbily, for she spent money on luxuries, and had to scrape up coppers for necessities. She thrived on gossip, but it was not delightfully scandalous gossip; it concerned the most minor incidents, in which no one but herself had any interest.

Mrs. Anderson was only friendly with Mrs. McKenzie because she needed someone to visit her occasionally and ease the loneliness of the house. The two women probably knew more about each other's affairs than their own families, and Mr. Anderson was jealous of Mrs. McKenzie. Occasionally he hinted at his dislike for her, but she always received his remarks dispassionately, and while she was visiting the house he was generally ignored, for Paul was occupied with Bryan.

Through the years the two boys had had about six violent arguments, which ended in their not seeing each other for months. The last one had been short, and, on Paul's part, unusually violent. He had been going out with Bryan for the whole of July and most of August, and they were no more discontented with each other than usual. One Friday night, they arranged to go to the pictures on the following Monday. They were to meet outside the cinema at seven o'clock.

Paul arrived in good time, but Bryan had still not come at half-past seven. Paul went into a phone box and rang the McKenzies' number. Mrs. McKenzie answered, and after a long delay, Paul finally heard Bryan's voice.

"You were supposed to meet me at seven o'clock," said Paul.

"That's too bad," said Bryan. He had committed himself to an argument, and he would not apologize, or admit that he had behaved badly. Temporarily, however, he was at a loss for words, and Paul had to ask, a little lamely. "Well, why didn't you come?"

"I went for a swim," replied Bryan, "and I wasn't back in time. It's too fine an evening to go to the pictures."

"How was I to know that you weren't coming?" asked Paul. "I've been waiting here for half an hour."

"That should do you good," said Bryan, "you don't get enough fresh air."

"Go to hell!" shouted Paul, and banged down the receiver. Afterwards he informed Bryan, through Mrs. McKenzie, that he had no wish to see him again. And to-night would be the first time they had seen each other for almost a year, for Mrs. McKenzie had sent Bryan to a boarding school in September, a few weeks after the argument. The worst thing about his arguments with Bryan, thought Paul, was that Mrs. McKenzie and Mrs. Anderson took them so seriously, and made them occasions for arguments of their own, whereas they should have appeared humorous. But then, old people had no sense of humour. After each argument, when his temper had cooled down, Paul laughed, and resolved that next time he would act in a more dignified manner. But he never did.

Bryan McKenzie had attended all the best schools in the town. He had been expelled from at least one of them, and suspended from several others. Mrs. McKenzie contended that the world had misused her son. He had always been misunderstood. When a window was broken, and Bryan was blamed for it, he had not even been in the vicinity at the time. And he was really a gentle soul, in spite of the numbers of books he had thrown at her and the pokers with which he had hit her, and the way all animals refused to come near him.

Paul did not blame Bryan for the way in which he behaved. Mrs. McKenzie was jealous of any other child of Bryan's age, and she was continually urging him to greater efforts at school, in the way he dressed, and the way he conducted himself. She was particularly jealous of Paul, for he was comfortably mediocre in the lower classes at school. Bryan had not passed an examination in his life, and he belittled Paul for scraping through them. Nevertheless, he envied Paul, and was ashamed of his own inability to concentrate on an academic subject for any length of time. He would have made a good craftsman, but Mrs. McKenzie would not hear of it. She was determined that Bryan should at least have a job at which he could wear clean clothes. She had not yet determined on the exact nature of the job; Paul imagined that she kept postponing the awful moment when she would have to face reality. A glance at Bryan's hands should have been enough to convince her of the futility of her ambitions for him: they were large and rough, with the skin blackened and torn, and the nails badly shaped. Paul's hands were comparatively white, with long fingers and soft skin.

Violence did not enter into Paul's relationship with Bryan. Paul refused to fight, for he knew quite well that he would be beaten. But Bryan was rather inarticulate, so when he was brutal Paul used sarcasm as a weapon, and he goaded Bryan into rages until he felt sure that he was going to strike him. After the first few days of one of their periods of friendship, they seldom had very much to say to each other, and when Paul was bored, he provoked Bryan to occupy the time. Their arguments were usually Paul's fault rather than Bryan's, although their parents did not realize it.

When they were very young they had good times together. They went swimming, on picnics into the countryside, and long hikes along the coast. They knew a hundred dark and secret places in the beautiful glen behind Paul's home. Very few people came to the glen, so in the middle of a clump of bushes they would build a hut with sticks and leaves. They supplied it with a larder and a bed, even a lavatory.

There was a river that ran through the glen, and at one point it had a high bank of earth beneath a shelf of rock. On the bank, above the level of the water, they built a hut. The river was overshadowed by trees, and when the sun shone behind their leaves in the late spring or early autumn, the light was pale green or deep gold, and it made patterns on their faces as they sat in silence, listening for the sound of footsteps on the path above them. No one could see them, and often they remained all day in the damp stillness, without saying a word.

One winter, when Paul was eight years old, there was a great storm, and a banana boat was wrecked on the rocks below the coast road. It was split in half, and one half drifted out to sea again, while the other sank gradually into the sand below the rocks. On the night when the ship was wrecked the people of the town flocked to salvage timber and bananas. Bryan and Paul arrived late next morning when there was only yellow scum left floating on the water. The ship had been wrecked a few yards from Jenny Watt's Cave.

One day a year later, when Bryan and Paul were out walking, they stopped to look down at the entrance to the cave.

It had been used by smugglers in the eighteenth century. A tunnel led from the entrance, under the town to another entrance miles away. As the years passed the tunnel was no longer used, and in parts it collapsed and became dangerous.

Suddenly the two boys noticed an object lying below them. The tide was coming in quickly, and it was just beginning to lap round the object. Bryan was much more daring than Paul, so he climbed down to the cave and picked up the object. Paul watched him bend down and look into the entrance of the cave. When he climbed back, he was holding a lantern. It had a wooden base and a wire frame.

"Perhaps it was used by smugglers in the old days," said Paul.

"Hardly," said Bryan. "There's an electric light built in it."

"Well then," said Paul, "perhaps it was used by modern smugglers."

Disregarding the remark, Bryan said, "It probably came from the ship that was wrecked."

Paul had read too many adventure stories to give up without a struggle. "I bet there's a priceless necklace hidden in the base," he said.

Bryan split the base with a stone. It was solid wood, and there was not even a hole where a necklace might have been hidden. They were very disappointed.

"What did the cave look like?" said Paul.

"That's a secret," said Bryan mysteriously, "but there was a dreadful smell . . . like dead, rotting bodies."

Paul was the only friend Bryan had, for he had attended so many schools that he had never been given the chance to make lasting friendships. It was rather hard for him to make friends, for at times he seemed strange to people who did not know him. Often he refused to answer when someone spoke to him, and when he was embarrassed he lapsed into baby-talk to attract attention and appear confident.

Paul imagined that Bryan behaved awkwardly because he felt inferior to other children: he had been adopted from an orphanage, and no one knew who his parents were. Mrs. McKenzie told him the truth one day when he was behaving badly, and afterwards she often reminded him of how grateful he should be to her. Of course, Paul was not supposed to know that Bryan was adopted, but Mrs. McKenzie could not keep a secret like that for very long.

One night Paul managed to introduce the subject of adoption. Bryan had been complaining about the treatment he received at home.

"Don't you wish you were adopted?" asked Paul. "Then you'd have no duty to your parents and you could do whatever you liked."

"I'd like to be adopted," said Bryan.

"Perhaps you are," said Paul.

"No such luck," said Bryan. Paul saw his face harden, and suddenly he felt very sorry for him.

Although Paul thought that he understood Bryan so well, there were times when he had to hold his strange manners up to ridicule, and try to make him angry.

Perhaps he had changed in a year.

Paul wondered if he still smoked cigars.

CHAPTER IV

WHEN Paul went downstairs, Mrs. McKenzie was sitting on the sofa, talking to Mrs. Anderson. Bryan was sitting alone in the opposite corner. As he closed the door, Paul said, "Hello, Mrs. McKenzie."

"Hello," she said, and glanced at him quickly and carefully. Paul made a remark on the weather, then after a few moments of silence Mrs. McKenzie began talking to Mrs. Anderson again.

Bryan acknowledged Paul with a slight movement of his mouth. Paul was not at all sure that the movement was intended to be friendly. Still standing by the door, he hesitated awkwardly. If he went into the scullery it would only delay the time when he would have to speak to Bryan. Finally, because Mrs. McKenzie and Mrs. Anderson were pretending not to watch him, he lifted a chair and carried it to where Bryan was sitting. The tension in the room relaxed a little, and the two women continued talking in low voices. Paul could not hear what they were saying, and that made him feel even more isolated.

Bryan was also embarrassed. Paul said, "Hello", a

second time, in a voice that was intended to be friendly. Unfortunately, it sounded rather cracked.

"You said that before," said Bryan. He was not the type of person to help anyone out of a difficulty.

"You haven't changed much, have you?" asked Paul. "You're still a drip." After that it was easy, and they were on the old terms of genial enmity. When Paul told him about his summer job, Bryan said that he was working in the hothouses of a nursery until the end of the summer. He had already started work. They discovered that they were both free in the evenings.

Paul said, "I'm sure you're going to apologize for what happened last summer."

Bryan pretended that he did not understand.

"Of course you understand," said Paul. He reminded him of the details of the argument.

"Really, Paul," said Bryan, "the language you used on the telephone that night was disgraceful. I was surprised at you."

Paul could not help smiling at his audacity. Bryan had never apologized to anyone, and he would not begin with Paul. Of course it was due to a deep hardness that was neither amusing nor assumed; it seemed strange that Paul should be sorry for him.

Paul said, "I suppose Mrs. McKenzie gave you a long lecture about behaving nicely to me?"

"Of course," said Bryan. His voice was rough, and had an assumed coarseness which meant that he never finished a word properly.

"I should have thought that by now she would have given up trying to reform you," said Paul.

"She's a bitch and a whore and a moron," said Bryan. Paul smiled, but he was careful not to agree with him, for he knew that Bryan might easily tell Mrs. McKenzie that Paul had called her a bitch and a whore and a moron.

"My mother hates you," said Bryan.

"Does she?" asked Paul. "Why did she bring you with her? In the hope that we'd have an argument?"

"No," said Bryan, "she was frightened that I might wreck the house while she was away."

By the time they sat down to tea, Bryan and Paul were allied against their parents. No matter what they said to each other in private, they resolved that they would support each other against older people. Paul did not tell Bryan about his hatred of being with other people, for he knew that Bryan would only regard it as another way of saying that he had lost all his friends.

Mr. Anderson arrived at the tea-table five minutes late. He had been gardening, and he had not changed into clean clothes. Paul saw that he was embarrassed. When he came into the room he said,

with an attempt at a smile, "So we've got visitors!"
Everyone knew that he must have heard the
McKenzies arriving. Mrs. McKenzie glanced at
him, then at Mrs. Anderson, who looked exas-
perated. Bryan was the only one who greeted him.
Paul thought that perhaps there was a great affinity
between his father and Bryan. They were misunderstood by most people, and neither of them was clever
enough to find a remedy.

When Mr. Anderson sat down at the table, he was
ignored. He stared glumly at the tablecloth, and his
eyelids twitched.

"What is Bryan going to do in September?" asked
Mrs. Anderson.

"I'm looking out for a suitable job at the moment," said Mrs. McKenzie.

"I want to join the Navy," said Bryan loudly.

"That's just what I should let you do," said his
mother shrilly. "You'd be in a fine position,
wouldn't you, away from home at your age."

There were times when she made no attempt to
hide her dissatisfaction with her adopted son, and
and others when she praised him highly. It all
depended on her mood, and she noticed no incon-
sistency between her reports.

"What are you going to do, Paul," she asked.

"I'm going to university," replied Paul, without
hesitation. "That is, if I pass my examination."

"Oh, indeed you will," said Mrs. McKenzie. "If everyone had as good a chance of passing as you have, they'd have no need to worry." She probably prayed every night that he would fail.

"I don't know," said Paul. "There were some of the examinations that I found very hard, and everyone else said they were easy."

Mrs. McKenzie looked hopeful. "You only imagine that," she said, but the words sounded faintly like a question. Mrs. Anderson would not hear failure mentioned, so she said, "I'm hoping that Paul will win a scholarship."

"You know I won't get one, Mother," said Paul. "I haven't a chance."

Mr. Anderson did not raise his eyes from the tablecloth. "Paul doesn't really want to go to university," he said.

There was a silence.

"Harry, that isn't true," said Mrs. Anderson.

His face reddened.

"It is true," said Paul. "I want to get a job in September, but my mother won't allow me." Mrs. McKenzie looked triumphant.

"Paul is going to university whether he likes it or not," said Mrs. Anderson. "I'm determined that he'll have a better position in life than his father."

Mrs. McKenzie launched her attack. "Well, I don't know, Mrs. Anderson," she said. "If Bryan didn't want to do a thing, I certainly wouldn't force him."

Bryan laughed shortly and loudly, and kicked Paul under the table. His mother ignored him.

"You know, Mrs. Anderson," she continued, "doing a thing like that might ruin the rest of Paul's life. If you take my advice you'll let him get a job if he wants to. Anyhow, a university education hasn't any particular value nowadays."

"And what kind of job could Paul obtain now?" asked Mrs. Anderson angrily. "A clerkship in an office?"

"I could get a job on a newspaper, or in an advertising agency," said Paul.

"You haven't still got those foolish notions of being an actor, have you, Paul?" asked Mrs. McKenzie hopefully.

"No," replied Paul. He thought that she had had quite enough pleasant news for one night.

They finished tea in almost complete silence. By a miracle, Mrs. Anderson somehow managed to make a few remarks in a normal voice. Bryan and Paul looked at each other meaningly, and Mr. Anderson seemed to relish the thought of the trouble he had caused. Finally, Mrs. Anderson invited Mrs. McKenzie out into the garden for the last of the sunshine. Paul asked Bryan to come for a walk. Mr. Anderson was left alone in the kitchen.

They decided to walk in the direction away from the town.

There were a few clouds around the setting sun, and it turned them to the sheerest gold. The golden light spread into the faint blue of the sky and grew paler every moment. The sea lapped round the coast, and the rocks jutting out from the shoreline. The ones in the foreground were silhouetted against the sky, for they were farthest from the sun. As they receded into the distance they grew bright, and were bathed in the wonderful glow. Then the sun made a line of light on the water. As it approached the shore it became broken on the rocks and seaweed.

In years to come, thought Paul, nights and days like this will be the only things that I remember about the summer when I did not understand myself. And I shall forget even these as I grow older.

Paul did not mention the beauty of the evening to Bryan. He knew that it would only embarrass him, although of all Paul's acquaintances he was the one who would best understand his emotion.

"I'm going to run away from home," said Bryan.

"Where are you going?" asked Paul.

"To sea," replied Bryan.

"I don't know why you think the sea is so romantic," said Paul. "It's just a lot of water."

"It's beautiful when there's a storm, and great waves, and a ship is tossed about on the ocean," said Bryan.

"Four hundred years ago," said Paul, "I should have felt the same as you do to-day. Then a voyage of discovery meant sailing to places that no European had ever seen before. But it's different now. A sea voyage is only a routine thing."

"There are still many places to be explored," said Bryan, "and I think there always will be."

"When are you leaving?" asked Paul, a little sarcastically.

"At the end of the summer," replied Bryan.

"Why not run away now?" asked Paul.

"I want to save up the money that I get for working in the nursery," said Bryan.

"Are you really so unhappy?" asked Paul.

"Of course I am," said Bryan. "You don't know what it's like, with my mother always urging me to do things, and gossiping, and comparing me with other boys."

Paul decided to trust him. "I'm unhappy too," he said "but I couldn't run away from home. It would be terrible to leave my mother all alone with my father. I'm all she has left in the world, and she planned for years that I should go to university. I can't disappoint her now."

"I can do whatever I like," said Bryan. "I have

no duty to my mother." He still called Mrs. McKenzie his mother.

"Remember the time you ran away before?" asked Paul. "Mrs. McKenzie made me look in all the huts that we had built, but it turned out that you had slept in the dog kennel during the night."

"I just did that to frighten her and gain attention," said Bryan. "Now I can't stand it any more. Why won't parents leave their children alone?"

"They're too selfish," replied Paul.

"Then aren't we being selfish in disobeying them?" asked Bryan.

"No," replied Paul, "our parents are being selfish with other people's lives. They use us for their own needs. They've had their lives, and they've made a mess of them, so they want to excuse themselves by making a success of our lives. Only they don't know what's best for us, so we'll be failures too."

Bryan said, "The only standard of success that our parents have is money."

"That's because they're poor," said Paul, "at least, my parents are poor."

"My mother never has any money either," said Bryan. "I don't know what she does with it."

"Perhaps when we are old," said Paul, "money will be our standard of success."

They walked on in silence for a time. Then Paul said, "If you run away from home, your mother will never have anything more to do with you. You'll have no home. You'll spend your life wandering from one place to another, and you'll never have anywhere to go back to. I think it would be sad to spend your life that way."

"I'd prefer that way to never having a moment's freedom," said Bryan.

"You'll have too much freedom," said Paul.

"Well, what do you want me to do?" shouted Bryan. "There is no middle way for me. I can either spend my life in a hell-hole with a bitch of a so-called mother, or I can run away and have nobody. What would you do?"

Paul turned away.

"I don't know," he said softly. "Perhaps someday you'll settle down somewhere, someday. Then you'll have roots. Oh, but please think about it carefully. It would be terrible to think of you being bitter and alone all your life. You'd become warped, and you'd always know that there was no one who loved you."

"Does anyone love you?" asked Bryan.

"No," replied Paul.

It was almost night time. They turned back towards the house.

"Are you coming out with me to-morrow night?" asked Paul.

"Yes," said Bryan. "Where shall we go?"

"The pictures?" asked Paul.

"All right," said Bryan, "we'll go there if it's a bad evening, but if the weather's good we'll go for a walk. Anyhow, I suppose we'll have another argument in a couple of weeks."

"Let's agree not to argue," said Paul. "If we get really fed up with each other, we can just give it up as a bad job, and we'll both understand. Then our parents won't have anything to talk about."

"No matter what we say," said Bryan, "we'll still have an argument sooner or later."

"We will not," said Paul. "Anyhow, call for me at the shop to-morrow night at seven."

When Bryan and Paul arrived home, their mothers were sitting in the kitchen.

"Where's father?" asked Paul.

"God knows," said Mrs. Anderson, "and I'm sure nobody cares." She turned to Mrs. McKenzie. "Does your husband ever take these fits of temper?" she asked. She knew what the answer would be.

"No," said Mrs. McKenzie, "he never loses his temper with me. He's one of the most placid men I've ever met."

"He isn't placid with me," interrupted Bryan loudly. "He was so angry with me yesterday that he nearly killed me."

"I never mentioned his behaviour to you, Bryan," said Mrs. McKenzie quickly. "No one could help losing their temper with you."

Bryan said, "I'm sure there are times when Father feels like hitting you over the head with something."

"If you say one more word," said Mrs. McKenzie, "we shall go home immediately. Why can't you do something quiet with Paul?"

His quietness was the only quality of Paul's that Mrs. McKenzie found praiseworthy. Paul sympathized with her. There were times when Bryan could have made a nervous wreck of a sensitive person. Not that Mrs. McKenzie was sensitive.

"Would you like to play poker?" asked Paul.

"Yes," replied Bryan, "for money."

"Of course," said Paul.

"You won't play poker in this house," said Mrs. Anderson, "you have enough vices as it is."

"Why do you object to poker?" asked Paul angrily.

"It's wrong," said Mrs. Anderson. She would have been incapable of elaborating on that statement.

"Oh, on religious grounds?" asked Paul sarcastically. "How long is it since you've been to church, even though you're always yapping at me to go?"

"I haven't time to go to church," said Mrs. Anderson. "You have. But you're not going to play poker."

"We've got nothing else to do," said Paul. "You entertain the few guests who ever come here badly enough ; you might at least let them enjoy themselves when they get the chance."

"Hear, hear !" said Bryan.

"Bryan !" exclaimed Mrs. McKenzie, "how dare you !"

"Go to your room at once, Paul," said Mrs. Anderson.

"All right, damn you," said Paul. "Come on, Bryan."

Bryan laughed uproariously, and shouting "Damn you, damn you !" he followed Paul out of the room. For a moment they listened outside the door. There was complete silence in the kitchen.

In his bedroom Paul brought out his cigarettes.

"No, thank you," said Bryan, "I have my cigars."

"You may have," said Paul quickly, "but you are not going to smoke them in my room. The smell of cigarettes is bad enough, but my mother would certainly notice the smell of cigars."

"What does it matter?" asked Bryan. "To hell with her."

"No," said Paul firmly. "Take a cigarette instead. Also, while we're on the subject of your disgusting habits, why do you put liquid paraffin on your hair?"

"I like it," said Bryan.

"Other people don't," said Paul. "Your hair looks dreadful."

"I don't care what other people think," said Bryan. Paul knew that he cared far too much what other people thought.

They lit their cigarettes, and sat in the dark with the window open.

"When you run away, which country will you visit first?" asked Paul.

"I'm going to take the first ship on which I can get a job," replied Bryan.

"Someday," said Paul, "I'm going to India, and China, and Africa : all the wonderful places that I've dreamed about for so long."

"Where are you going to get the money?" asked Bryan. "You love comfort too much to live in poverty."

"I'd like to travel, even more than I like comfort," said Paul.

"My mother laughs at ambitions like these," said Bryan. "She says that when you finally visit all the lands you've dreamed about, you'll be very disappointed."

"I should never be disappointed," said Paul. "It depends on yourself whether or not you think the land is beautiful. Some people, like our parents, are incapable of seeing beauty."

"I wonder if all children think so little of their parents as we do?" asked Bryan.

"Not if they're rich, and they have a nice home

and a pleasant future to look forward to," said Paul. "I wish I had a great talent, like being a brilliant scientist, or writer, or a talented musician."

"Perhaps you would have been a wonderful actor," suggested Bryan.

"Hardly," said Paul. "If I were destined to be a great actor then surely I should let nothing stand in my way; I shouldn't stop to consider my mother's unhappiness."

"Well, you're quite a good pianist," said Bryan. "Why don't you practise hard at that?"

"I never really wanted to learn the piano," replied Paul. "And lately I've grown to hate it. Besides, I don't like classical music."

"I'm even less talented than you are," said Bryan. "There's nothing I could do to make a lot of money and become famous. Anyhow I don't want to be famous."

"You could become a good engineer," said Paul, "if your mother would allow you."

"She wouldn't consider it," said Bryan. "And I can't live with her any longer."

"Bryan," said Paul, "when you leave home write to me and tell me all about the things you're doing. I promise not to show the letters to Mrs. McKenzie."

"All right," said Bryan, "but they'll be very short letters. I'm not good at writing."

They sat in the room for another hour, smoking in silence. Then Mrs. McKenzie called Bryan's name. Paul did not go down to see him off. As he went out of the room, Bryan said, "I'll see you to-morrow night. Don't tell your mother you're going out with me."

From the window Paul watched him leaving with Mrs. McKenzie. Paul could well imagine what she was saying to him, and he decided that he would face Mrs. Anderson immediately. He went downstairs to make his supper.

His mother was waiting for him. As soon as he went into the kitchen, she said, "That was a fine display in front of Mrs. McKenzie. You should be ashamed of yourself."

"I'm not in the least ashamed," said Paul. "It was your stupid prudery that started the argument. You know that you've no religious principles."

"I can remember a time when you yourself thought playing poker was wrong," said Mrs. Anderson. "You've changed a lot since then."

"I know I have," said Paul. "I've grown up a little."

"Then God help you," said Mrs. Anderson.

Paul wanted to shock her. "There is no God," he sneered. "He's only a myth made up for the sake and convenience of bloody fools like you."

Mrs. Anderson began crying. When he saw a

woman crying, Paul usually felt uncomfortable, but this time he did not care at all.

"It's Bryan McKenzie who has put all these ideas in your head," said Mrs. Anderson. "I forbid you to see him again."

"You can't stop me," said Paul. "I'll see him if I want to."

"I'll bring the minister to see you," sobbed Mrs. Anderson, "you can't go on like this."

Paul laughed. "What good do you think he can do?" he asked. "I'm not afraid of him like you and Father are." Paul paused, and when his mother did not reply, he continued, "You say that it's a sin to swear and play poker. Do you not realize that it's a greater sin to talk about your husband the way you talked about him to-night? Do you never realize that it's at least partly your fault that he has such a bad temper? Yet you sit and relate all his faults to Mrs. McKenzie, knowing that she'll have told half the people of the town by the next day."

As Paul finished, Mr. Anderson came into the room. "I could hear your voices when I was in the garden," he said. "Did you not argue enough with the McKenzies to-night?"

"No," said Paul. "What business is it of yours?" His father turned white with anger.

"It's all my business," he shouted. "Go to bed before I knock the living daylights out of you."

Paul could easily have beaten his father in a fight, but he felt very tired; he hesitated, and then went upstairs.

Why do I act like this when I know it's no use, he wondered. No matter what I do or say, my parents will never change. They'll go on like this until the day they die. If only I had been born into a happy home, just a normal one where my parents still loved each other, and they only had occasional arguments about petty things . . . and they loved me.

From now on I'll have as little to do with them as possible. I won't show my feelings, I won't care, I'll be cool and detached. But I'll try not to become like Bryan.

CHAPTER V

B RYAN called for Paul at seven o'clock the next
evening, and they left the shop immediately.

"What did your mother say to you last night?"
asked Paul.

"She yapped at me all the way home," replied
Bryan, "and she says that you're a bad influence on
me. She said that she wouldn't allow me to go out
with you again."

"What did you say?" asked Paul.

"I told her to go to hell."

"Don't tell her that you were out with me this
evening," warned Paul, "or she'll tell my mother.
I told my mother this morning that I wouldn't
go out with you again. I had to .apologize for
last night, or she'd never have stopped talking
about it."

"All right," said Bryan. "Where do you want to
go to-night?"

"The pictures," replied Paul.

"I don't," said Bryan. "We agreed that if it was a
fine evening we'd go for a walk. I want to find a girl
friend."

"I'm not going to help you find one," said Paul quickly.

"Why not?" asked Bryan. "You used to be crazy about girls. Remember Rosemary?"

"I'll never forget her," said Paul. "If I ever see the bitch again I'll seduce her."

Bryan laughed heavily. "Good for you," he said. "Why did you stop seeing her?"

"She was beginning to get too cocksure of herself," said Paul. "She thought that I'd come running every time she called."

"I bet you wouldn't seduce her," said Bryan.

"How much?" asked Paul.

"Nothing," replied Bryan. "You'd have no proof: I couldn't very well watch you while you were doing it."

"I shouldn't mind," said Paul, "although Rosemary might."

"Why don't we try and find her to-night," asked Bryan. "She could bring a friend for me."

Paul was already bored with Bryan's company, so he agreed. It should be fun trying to seduce Rosemary, although he felt no particular urge.

"I'll go and ring her up," he said. Bryan rubbed his hands in anticipation. "You must be sexually frustrated," said Paul. Bryan made a face.

The last Paul had seen of Rosemary was about six months ago. He told her then that he would ring her up some time, so he was only fulfilling a promise. "Soon," she had whispered in his ear, before the last kiss. Now that he thought about it, Paul realized that Rosemary had often tried to seduce him.

It was Rosemary's mother who answered the phone.

"Is Rosemary there?" asked Paul.

"Yes," said Mrs. Bates' deep voice. "Who shall I say is calling?"

"A friend," replied Paul coldly. Mrs. Bates disliked him. She was a large, muscular woman.

"Hello," said Rosemary huskily.

"This is Paul." He made his voice smoulder with as much suppressed passion as possible.

"Oh," said Rosemary.

"How are you?" asked Paul.

"Quite well," said Rosemary, "considering."

"Would you like to meet me this evening?" asked Paul. There was a pause.

"I'd love to," said Rosemary, "but I've already arranged to go out. With a girl," she added quickly.

She had no pride, thought Paul.

"I'm with a male friend," he said, "so you can bring your friend along and we'll make up a foursome."

"All right," said Rosemary enthusiastically. "Who is your friend?"

"Bryan McKenzie," replied Paul.

"Are you going around with him again?" asked Rosemary. The words conveyed a subtle compliment, that Paul was superior to a person like Bryan.

"What's the name of your friend?" asked Paul.

"Mary Gordon," replied Rosemary. "You don't know her, she's just on holiday. She isn't good looking, but she's a *nice* girl."

"We'll call for you in half an hour," said Paul. "I'll be seeing you."

"Good-bye, Paul," she said.

Rosemary's friend Mary had a country accent, a high-pitched voice, a pale face, and a good figure. Bryan was very contented with her. They met outside Rosemary's house, and after the introductions, they split into two pairs. Paul and Rosemary walked a little in front of Bryan and Mary.

Paul glanced back occasionally, and he saw that Bryan was resting his hand lightly on Mary's shoulder. Paul had his hand round Rosemary's waist. As they walked along, Rosemary frequently moved his hand up a little, towards her breast.

She was an attractive girl, and she could have had many boy-friends. Paul could not imagine why she had chosen him. She had glistening dark hair, a baby face, well made up, and she was a little top-heavy. Her only fault was her habit of dramatizing every action and speech. Paul noticed it because he was too sensitive. When he was with Rosemary for any length of time, she made him feel slightly insane.

"I missed you, Paul," she said huskily.

"Have you been smoking?" he asked.

She had no sense of humour.

"No," she replied, "I believe that it's unladylike for girls to smoke. Why didn't you come to see me sooner?"

"I was working for my examinations," lied Paul.

"I'm sure you'll do very, very well," said Rosemary enthusiastically.

"Where do you want to go to-night?" asked Paul.

"I don't mind," she said.

"Do you want to come for a walk?"

"Yes."

She moved his hand a little nearer her breast.

Paul looked back at Bryan and Mary. "We're going for a walk," he said. "Where are you going?"

"We'll follow you," replied Bryan.

Paul had been afraid of that. He smiled half-heartedly, and turned back to Rosemary.

They reached the promenade. Hundreds of couples like themselves were walking along slowly, with their arms around each other.

"Let's go in and get an ice-cream," said Paul.

"I'd love one," said Rosemary.

They joined the queue that led into the shop. As they waited they idly watched the crowds on the promenade. Suddenly Paul saw Gary, with another boy of his own age. Gary glanced at the queue; he spoke to his friend, and they joined it. They were standing behind Bryan and Mary, and if they had talked to one another, Paul could have heard what they said. The queue reached the interior of the shop. Paul looked into the mirror behind the counter, and straight into Gary's eyes. He was startled, and his expression must have betrayed him, for Gary looked amused, and turned back to his friend, smiling. Paul flushed.

Very deliberately, he put his hand firmly on Rosemary's breast. She breathed heavily and came closer to him. When they had bought their ices, they left the shop. Out of the corner of his eye, Paul could see Gary watching him. Damn Gary, he thought, why should I care what he thinks about me? The way I'm acting anyone would think I was a fruit. Gary probably is. He looks like one.

"Rosemary," he said nervously, "why don't we go for a walk in the glen behind my home?"

"If you want to, Paul," she said softly.

Paul sweated. He thought that he must be

green with nerves. And Bryan and Mary followed, at a discreet distance, all the way to the glen. Paul smoked cigarettes until he felt sick. God, he thought, I wish this was over. Rosemary did not betray the slightest trace of nervousness.

They found a small field. Bryan and Mary sat down in one corner, and Paul and Rosemary lay down in another. The remaining two corners were also occupied. Paul kissed Rosemary immediately, then stretched his body against hers. She was obviously entertained, and somehow she managed to twist her legs around Paul's. He began feeling her breasts, and then he opened her dress at the back and took off her brassière. Her breasts were soft and warm, and he was actually able to work up some enthusiasm. Rosemary lay still most of the time, but she wriggled occasionally, when she felt that Paul's interest might be waning.

"Oh, Paul," she whispered, with what he supposed was genuine passion. "This is what I've been waiting for. Do you love me?"

"Yes, Rosemary," he replied dutifully and squeezed one of her breasts. When she had recovered from the ecstasy of that, she said, "Paul, you can do this as often as you want to."

"Thank you, Rosemary," he said. "How far are you going to let me go?"

"What do you mean?" she asked coyly.

Paul felt like getting up and running, but instead he put his hand between her legs.

"Oh no Paul," she said unconvincingly. "I don't think people should do that until they're married." She waited.

"But Rosemary darling," said Paul, "we can't get married for a long time yet. Surely you don't want to wait too long?"

"No," she breathed.

"I'm sunk," thought Paul.

When it was over, he felt completely disgusted. He pushed her away, and sat up.

"It's ten o'clock," he said. "We'd better go."

Mary was lying with her head on Bryan's lap, and Bryan was watching Paul admiringly.

"Just one more kiss," said Rosemary.

"No," said Paul. "I don't want more kisses, or anything else. I didn't even find making love to you very pleasant."

It took at least two minutes for Rosemary to recover from the shock. "You can't do this to me," she said at last, without the slightest notion that she was being corny.

"Who's going to stop me?" asked Paul coldly.

"Damn you, damn you," shrieked Rosemary, and she began crying.

"Look, Rosemary," said Paul, "you got what you

wanted, didn't you? It was a first-class seduction, but if ever I do it with another girl, I'd like to be the one who does the seducing. I don't love you, I'm certainly not going to marry you, I didn't even want to come out with you to-night. I did it for a bet. You obviously enjoyed yourself, so why not leave it at that. I won't be seeing you again."

Rosemary was trying to have hysterics, but so far she had been unsuccessful.

"I hate you," she cried, "what happens if I have a baby?"

"You know as well as I do that you won't have a baby," said Paul impatiently. He lit his last cigarette.

Bryan came over. "Are you coming soon, Paul?" he asked.

"I'll go straight into the house if you don't mind taking Rosemary home," said Paul. "Unless you'd like to come in for a night-cap."

"I'd prefer to take Mary straight home," said Bryan. He looked at Rosemary without enthusiasm. "Coming, Rosemary?" he asked.

"In a minute," she whispered heart-brokenly. She was going to have great fun playing tragedy for the next few weeks.

"If you don't mind I'll go on," said Paul. "My parents will be expecting me. I'll be seeing you, Bryan." He hesitated. "Good luck, Rosemary," he said. She gave no indication that she had heard him. She sat gazing in front of her, with rather short-sighted eyes.

Paul walked home listlessly, and went up to his room on tip-toe, so that his parents would not hear him. Then taking a towel, he went out again, down to the beach.

He stripped off his clothes, and ran completely naked out to sea.

The moon shone brilliantly on the water, but he was terrified by the darkness beneath him. He moved restlessly in the water, with a sick feeling in his stomach. Self-consciously, he began praying for forgiveness to the god in whom he had no belief. "Oh God, I'm sorry for what I did to-night, but I was too proud to break away. Forgive and give me peace. Give me happiness, and friends whom I love and trust. Give me something to live for." Perhaps Paul really desired these things, but his prayer was hollow, and the sentences were meaningless when they were addressed to God.

Paul began to have the feeling that he had when he smoked his first cigarette. Waves of nausea swept over him, and he felt alternately hot and cold. He began vomiting into the sea, and his mouth and nose were filled with sourness. He retched again and again, and each time he prayed that it would be the last.

When it was over, he swam towards the beach again, and washed out his mouth with sea-water. He even swallowed some of it. He felt weak, and he just managed to reach the shore. He staggered up the sand, and into the house. There was still no one about. In his room, he lay down on the bed. At first he had not even enough energy to pull the clothes over him. Finally, he slipped between the sheets, and went to sleep.

CHAPTER VI

I

GARY came into the shop next morning. He bought some cigarettes, but he gave no sign that he was aware of Paul's existence, except as a shop-assistant. While he went to get the change, Paul left the book he had been reading lying on the counter. When he came back, he saw that Gary had picked up the book, and was looking at it. Paul, at a loss for what to say, put the change on the rubber mat. Gary looked up, and flushed.

"I'm sorry," he said. His voice was kind, and rather nervous.

"It's all right," said Paul. "You can go on reading it if you want to."

He was glad that Gary could be embarrassed. He had thought of him as proud and invulnerable, and he liked him more when he realized that he had been wrong.

"I've already read the book" said Gary. "It's just that I was surprised to find *you* reading it."

"Why?" asked Paul coldly.

85

Gary grew even more embarrassed.

"Well," he stammered, "shop-assistants don't usually read Plato."

"Neither do factory workers," said Paul.

"I'm not a factory worker," said Gary. "I'm only working there for the summer."

"And I'm not a shop-assistant," said Paul. "I'm only working here for the summer."

They began laughing.

"I'm sorry," said Gary.

"I'm not," said Paul. "I knew that you'd only taken a summer job. One of the girls told me."

After a moment, Gary said, "I'm still wondering about your reading Plato. Is he your idea of entertainment?"

"No," said Paul. "I'm reading him to improve my mind."

"Does it need improving so badly?" asked Gary.

"I'm afraid it does," replied Paul. "Why do you read him?"

Gary laughed again. "To improve my mind," he said.

There was an awkward pause. Paul expected him to leave the shop, but he remained, although he kept his eyes on the floor and did not speak.

"Haven't you enough medical books to read?" asked Paul.

"I think I should also have some knowledge of

great literature," said Gary seriously. Then he looked surprised. "How did you know that I was studying medicine?" he asked.

"Mr. Swallow told me."

Again they lapsed into silence, but still Gary did not seem to want to leave.

"Do you work hard at university?" asked Paul.

"Yes," replied Gary, "very hard." He looked solemn.

"You take yourself very seriously, don't you?" said Paul.

Gary looked wary, as if he was afraid that Paul might be laughing at him.

"Yes," he said.

"I'm glad," said Paul. "So few people do nowadays, and the others seem to be ashamed to admit it. They seem to think that people will laugh at them."

"That's exactly the way I feel," said Gary. He paused, and smiled uncertainly, "I'd better go," he said, "but I'll be in again."

Paul smiled. "Good-bye," he said.

Then he thought about his conversation with Gary. Gary was shy, he was not at all proud. Perhaps the reason that he never spoke before was that he was just as shy as Paul.

If only he could become my friend, thought Paul. But then he must be very popular, with many friends, and he'll be quite happy with them. Besides, he belongs to a different class, and he's much older, and more intelligent than I am.

For the rest of the day Paul thought about Gary, and imagined what it would be like to know him well. He did not consider it at all strange that he should think about Gary so much, although he did not even know his real name. At tea-time he watched the workers coming out of the factory, hoping that Gary would go into the café. But he went in the opposite direction, without a glance across at the shop, and Paul ate his tea alone. Mr. Swallow repeated his invitation to tea in his house, but he had given Paul potatoes and bacon every day, and Paul decided that he would be better eating at the café.

II

When Paul arrived home in the evening, Bryan rang up. Mrs. Anderson answered the telephone, and she remained in the hall to hear what Paul said.

"Congratulations," said Bryan, "you did very well last night."

"I'm not very proud of it," said Paul.

"You certainly didn't treat Rosemary very well afterwards," said Bryan. "She walked home with

Mary and me, with a dazed look and her mouth hanging open like a goldfish."

"Don't worry about her," said Paul. "She enjoyed herself immensely. How did you get on with Mary?"

"Quite well," said Bryan, "but she had more inhibitions than Rosemary."

"You don't know how lucky you are," said Paul. "All day I've felt as if someone was hitting me on the head with a hammer."

Mrs. Anderson looked anxious.

"Are you coming out to-night?" asked Bryan.

"No," replied Paul. "I'm not allowed to come out with you again."

Mrs. Anderson nodded her head in satisfaction, and went into the kitchen.

"I'm sorry about that," said Paul, "my mother was listening. She's gone now."

"The old bitch," said Bryan.

"I know she's a bitch," said Paul, "but you must be a bugger or you wouldn't call her one. But Bryan, I won't be coming out with you again. What I did last night was wrong. You know I don't believe in religion any more, but afterwards I felt filthy. Rosemary is probably taking it more seriously than I've pretended, but there's nothing I can do about it. If I go to her and apologize, she'll think that she does mean something to me, after all."

Bryan understood.

"You're probably right," he said. "I won't be seeing Mary again, I had enough of her last night. But that doesn't mean that you can't come out with me."

"If I go out with you," said Paul, "we'll get bored again, like we did last night, and we'll argue until finally one of us agrees to do something that he doesn't really want to do. And afterwards he'll be sorry. I haven't anything against you, you're the only real friend I ever had. If you leave home, write to me. I'd like to know how you get on."

"Very well," said Bryan slowly. "What are you going to do with yourself for the rest of the summer?"

"I don't know," said Paul, "but I won't be going out with any of my so-called friends. I'd prefer to be alone. I'll read a few books, go swimming . . . " He could not think of anything else, so he added, "I may even smoke and drink myself sick."

"Don't," said Bryan, and Paul heard him put down the receiver. It was a strange good-bye, but completely in keeping with their relationship. For a while Paul stood in the hall, gazing about him helplessly, then he went into the sitting-room, and sat down at the piano. With his right hand, he picked out a tune on the keys. The room was warm and silent, and the piano needing tuning, so that the music seemed to have an echo. Paul felt very lonely.

Suddenly he heard the kitchen door being flung open, and his mother's voice calling, "Paul, Paul!" He went into the hall. "Come quickly," said Mrs. Anderson, "Harry's ill."

Mr. Anderson was stretched out on the kitchen floor. Blood was trickling from a cut on his forehead. Paul went over to him. He was unconscious.

"Help me to get him on to the sofa," said Paul. His mother was trembling, and he was of little use, but finally they managed to lift Mr. Anderson from the floor. "Get a wet cloth," said Paul. His mother rushed into the scullery, looking back over her shoulder.

Mr. Anderson's face was very white, and his cheeks looked hollow. He opened his eyes. He did not know where he was, or what had happened to him.

"Lie still," said Paul. "I'm going to get the doctor."

"No," said Mr. Anderson, "I'll be all right." He tried to sit up.

"Lie back," said Paul, firmly, "you must be quiet."

When Mrs. Anderson came back with the cloth, Paul dabbed it on the cut on his father's forehead. The skin was only slightly opened, although it was bleeding freely.

"Ring up the doctor," Paul said to his mother. "For God's sake tell him to hurry." He knew that she was so nervous that she might do anything if he left her alone with her husband.

"I don't need a doctor, Paul," said Mr. Anderson. "Please don't bring one." Paul noticed that the lines of sarcasm and bad-temper around his father's mouth were still there, although now he was weak and pleading.

"You need a doctor," said Paul. "If he comes, you'll soon be all right."

Mr. Anderson relaxed a little. Paul felt curiously detached from the scene. He had no feelings towards his father. He knew exactly what he had to do, and otherwise he didn't care.

"I'm sorry I fainted," said Mr. Anderson. "That's what happened, isn't it?"

"I think so," said Paul.

His mother came back into the kitchen. "The doctor's coming as soon as he can," she said. She sat on the arm of the sofa.

"What happened?" asked Paul softly.

"I was working in the scullery," she said, "when I heard a groan. When I went into the kitchen, Harry was swaying on his feet, and holding on to the mantelpiece. Then he toppled over, and as he fell his head hit the arm of the chair." Her mouth trembled. "Oh, God, Paul, what's going to happen to him?" she cried. Paul felt awkward. He hated to see his mother when she was upset.

"Don't disturb him, Mother," he pleaded.

The doctor did not arrive for over an hour, and during that time Mr. Anderson fainted three times. Mrs. Anderson cried hysterically, and finally she had to go up to her room. Paul sat watching his father's sick, ugly face, resting on the blankets. It occurred to him that his mother might possibly love his father, although she had had a strange way of showing it.

When the doctor came, she showed him into the kitchen, and then she shouted at him: "What kept you? Harry might be dead by now. But you took your time, you didn't care. If Harry dies, I'll take you to every court in the country."

The doctor ignored her. He examined Mr. Anderson carefully, and when he had finished, he said to Paul: "Help me to carry him up to his bedroom." Mrs. Anderson followed them, and watched them as they undressed her husband and put him to bed.

"You can leave him alone for a minute," said the doctor. "I want to speak to you."

Paul led his mother out of the room, and stood with her on the landing, as the doctor came out, and closed the door. Paul held his mother's arm, and he could feel it shaking.

"Is Harry going to die?" she asked.

"Yes," said the doctor. "He's had a stroke. There's nothing I can do for him."

Mrs. Anderson whimpered.

"How long will he live?" asked Paul.

"I don't know," said the doctor. "A few days, perhaps even a number of weeks."

"This is all so sudden," said Paul helplessly. "I never dreamed that my father wouldn't live for at least a few more years."

"I know, son," said the doctor, without undue sympathy. "It'll take a while getting used to it. Have you got a friend who can look after your mother?"

"Yes," replied Paul. "I'll ring her up."

"Good," said the doctor. "I'll leave a prescription at the chemists, and I'll come to-morrow, and see how he is."

Paul watched him leave the house, and then he phoned Mrs. McKenzie. It was Bryan who answered.

"This is Paul. Can I speak to your mother? It's urgent."

Paul heard Bryan start to speak, then he must have changed his mind, for Paul could hear the noise as he laid the receiver on the table.

"Is there something wrong?" asked Mrs. McKenzie when she came.

"Yes," said Paul. "My father's had a stroke, and

the doctor says that he's going to die. Can you come and look after my mother?"

"Of course," said Mrs. McKenzie immediately. "I'll come at once."

"Thank you," said Paul. "On your way, will you collect a prescription at the chemist's?"

"Yes," she said. "I'll send Bryan for it. I won't be long. Good-bye."

"Good-bye," said Paul.

His mother had gone back into his father's room. She was sitting on the bed, crying quietly. Paul left her there. He could not bear the thought of having to comfort her. It was something at which he was not very good. He went to his room, and lit a cigarette. He could not think very clearly.

His father was going to die. There would be a funeral, but it would be a very small one, for he had not many friends. But afterwards the house would be crowded with chattering people, enjoying a cup of tea, and a talk with relations whom they did not see very often.

Damn the bloody lot of them.

Only they could not love Mr. Anderson any less than Paul did. Well, it was not his fault. He wanted to love as much as anyone, but he could not love an ugly bad-tempered fool. Seemingly his mother did love her husband, but she had known him when he was young, before he became warped and stupid.

Paul was not sorry that his father was dying, but he was angry that there would be a delay. If he died immediately, the funeral would be over in a couple of days, and then they could get back to normal. Only the house would be so much more peaceful; there would be fewer arguments, Paul would be happier.

Perhaps Mrs. Anderson was only acting the shortly-to-be bereaved wife, but Paul did not think so. She must be remembering her husband as he used to be, and her love was returning through the years, and it was as if she had just been married. She was lucky, she had been in love for a time. When she was young, she was rich, and attractive and happy. She could afford to be headstrong. She had nothing to complain about. If she expected any more from life she was being ungrateful for what she had already received. She had been given her share of happiness.

Of course now Paul was beginning to realize that he did not want his father to die but that was too bad; he was going to die and that was all there was to that. Well, Paul's regret would not last for long, and afterwards he would be glad that he had peace at last. If he thought otherwise, he was a bloody bloody fool.

Mrs. McKenzie came in less than half an hour. Paul was sincere when he thanked her for coming.

"Try and stop my mother from being hysterical

in front of Father," he said. "He's just about conscious, and he'll realize why she's behaving like that. If I can, I'd like to talk to him alone for a while."

"Of course, Paul," said Mrs. McKenzie. Her eyes were kind.

Paul thought that he was not a very wise person. Forty-eight hours ago he had treated Mrs. McKenzie as a figure of fun, believing that she had not a decent feeling in her body. But in a time of real trouble she was kind. It was only that she was like the rest of the people that he knew intimately: a victim of circumstances. Surely somewhere there is a world different from this, thought Paul. I've read about it in books and seen it in films, and it was taken for granted that it was normal. But I know my own world best, and I think it must be the normal one. All my life I shall be running away from the things that have happened to me this year and all the years I can remember, and I shall be trying to change myself to someone else.

When Paul led Mrs. McKenzie into the room where his father was lying, Mrs. Anderson was considerably quietened, and she did not resist when Mrs. McKenzie suggested that it would be better if she went down to the kitchen. Paul sat down on the bed.

His father's eyes were open, but they had a glazed look.

"Father, do you recognize me?" asked Paul.

"Yes," he whispered. His lips were dry and cracked. "Am I going to die, Paul?" he asked.

"Yes," said Paul.

"Oh God," said his father, "I don't want to die."

"It will probably be very peaceful," said Paul. "There will be no more worries or troubles."

"Do you believe in heaven?" asked Mr. Anderson.

"No, Father," said Paul. "There will just be utter silence and peace."

"I'm glad," said Mr. Anderson, attempting to smile. "I always thought that heaven would be very dull if I spent eternity singing psalms."

After a moment he continued, "I'm sorry, Paul. I haven't been a very good father."

"I haven't been a very good son," said Paul.

"It was my fault, Paul," he said.

Paul knew exactly what he meant.

"I know," he said. "I understand. Very few people can be good. In a way, it's a little pointless to try."

"I want to give you some advice," said Mr. Anderson. "When I die, I want you to do exactly as you like. Don't waste your life listening to other people, or you'll be very unhappy. It doesn't matter what anyone else says or does."

"I shall always listen to other people," said Paul.

His father tried to smile again. "I know," he said, "you aren't strong enough."

"Did you love my mother?" asked Paul.

"In a way," replied Mr. Anderson.

"Do you love me?"

"Yes."

"I shall always remember that," said Paul. And he watched his father fall asleep. He was breathing very lightly, and for a while Paul watched the gentle rise and fall of the bedclothes about his body. Then he left the room.

When Paul went downstairs, Bryan had arrived with the prescription, and Mrs. McKenzie was preparing it. Mrs. Anderson was sitting quietly in a chair. She seemed almost normal again, but she was white-faced.

"Come up to my room, Bryan," said Paul. "I'd like to talk to you."

As they went upstairs, Bryan asked, "Is your father really going to die, Paul?"

"Yes," said Paul.

"When?"

"Within a few weeks, at the longest."

"Are you sorry?"

"For some things," said Paul, "but he's going to be much happier."

"I liked him," said Bryan.

"I'll probably be seeing quite a lot of you, after all," said Paul, "if Mrs. McKenzie is going to come and look after my mother. She'll certainly need someone in the house."

"What are you going to do now?" asked Bryan.

"My father's death changes very little," said Paul.

"Are you still going to university?"

"Yes," replied Paul, "my mother will probably be more determined than ever about that."

There was little more to say. Paul did not really want to talk to Bryan, he just wanted to be with someone. They sat in the room in the dark, and the only light was the moonlight and the glow of their cigarettes.

But how much more wonderful the silence would be if Gary were sitting opposite me, thought Paul.

Presently, Mrs. McKenzie knocked at the door.

"I've arranged to stay for the night, Paul," she said. "Bryan can go home."

"Do you think I'll be able to go to work in the morning?" asked Paul. The kindness that he had discovered in Mrs. McKenzie made him want to trust her, and let her make decisions for him.

"I expect you can go to work" she said, " if your father isn't any worse. You can't stay away from work indefinitely, and once or twice during the day you can ring up and make sure that you're not needed."

"Thank you," said Paul, "for all you're doing to help us."

She flushed with pleasure. "I'm very pleased to help you, Paul," she said awkwardly.

Paul left Bryan part of the way home, before returning to the house.

"You're going to be lonely, Bryan," said Paul, "if your mother is staying with us for a while."

"There's a girl in the office at the nursery," said Bryan. "I think I'll ask her to go out with me."

"I'm glad," said Paul. "Enjoy yourself this summer, no matter what you're going to do in the autumn."

"Why do you give that advice to me," asked Bryan, "when you yourself aren't going to have a good time?"

"I can hardly have a good time, can I?" asked Paul. "Anyhow, the things that you like doing don't make me happy."

"What does make you happy?" asked Bryan.

"I don't know," said Paul. But privately he thought that if he could spend the summer with Gary he would be very, very happy.

As he went to bed that night, he looked in on his father, who was sleeping; but he avoided his mother. He had noticed that as she grew calmer, the hardness in her nature once more became apparent. Before he went to sleep, he thought a lot about Gary, and very little about his father. He had almost finished with him now, and the pity and regret were already beginning to fade away. He knew that it was wrong, but there was nothing he could do about it.

CHAPTER VII

I

WHEN he arrived at work next morning Paul told Mr. Swallow about his father.

"How is he now?" asked Mr. Swallow.

"Just the same as last night," said Paul. "He certainly doesn't seem to be any worse."

He was surprised that Mr. Swallow did not show more sympathy, but then nothing seemed to surprise or upset him unduly.

"What age were you when your parents died?" asked Paul.

"I was eight when my father died," replied Mr. Swallow, "and I was fifteen when my mother died."

"Did you have to go to work immediately?" asked Paul.

"I wasn't forced to," replied Mr. Swallow. "My mother left me a little money, enough to buy my shop and house with. But I was too young to start out on my own, so I took a job in a large shop and learnt the trade. I bought this shop when I was twenty-five, and I've been here ever since."

"Did you never think of marrying?" asked Paul.

"I thought of it," replied Mr. Swallow. He cleared his throat. "I never met the right girl."

"Then do you approve of marriage, in principle at least?" asked Paul.

"For some people," said Mr. Swallow. "Some people are lucky."

For the rest of the day, Paul tried to concentrate on a French novel which was supposed to be one of the most famous ever written. Paul found it unutterably boring, but that was because he gave it only part of his attention. Often he glanced across the road at the factory, but he did not see Gary, not even at lunchtime, for all the employees had their lunch in the factory. Then, at teatime, a shadow fell across his book, and when he looked up he saw Gary standing in the doorway.

"Hello," he said, with a smile that was still a little uncertain.

"Hello," said Paul.

Gary bought cigarettes again, in another twenty packet.

"Do you smoke very many cigarettes?" asked Paul.

"Unfortunately, yes," said Gary. "About twenty a day."

"I smoke almost as many," said Paul. "It's far too many, and I can't really afford it."

Gary pretended that he was going to leave the shop, then stopped, and said, as though the thought had just entered his head,

"You aren't by any chance having your tea in the café across the road?" he asked.

"Yes, I am," said Paul.

"Would you like to have it with me?" asked Gary.

"I'd love to," said Paul.

He saw that Gary's pleasure was entirely frank and genuine.

As Gary began eating his meal, Paul took the opportunity of studying him more closely.

His skin had become a little darker since the time when Paul studied him at church. His eyes were hazel coloured, and his teeth were white and fine. His finger nails were a little ragged: he worked hard. He had no wristwatch.

He's exactly the way I'd like to be when I'm his age, thought Paul.

"You know, I don't even know your name," said Paul.

"John," he said. "John Knight."

The name did not register on Paul. The name of the boy sitting opposite was still "Gary".

"Well, mine is Paul Anderson," he said.

"I know," said Gary.

"How?" asked Paul, surprised.

"Someone told me years ago," said Gary, "when you used to sit behind me in church. Why did you stop going? I don't even see you at Communion now."

"It's a long story," said Paul.

"I'm sorry," said Gary.

"I should like to tell you sometime," said Paul hastily, "but not just now."

"All right," said Gary, "I'll hold you to your promise."

Paul hesitated, then he said, "I didn't know your real Christian name, and I had to call you something, so I made up a name for you—Gary."

Gary thought for a while. He looked amused.

"I like that name," he said. "You can call me Gary if you want to."

"Good," said Paul. "I should have thought of you as Gary, anyhow."

Gary said casually, "You don't by any chance know what's on at the pictures this week, do you?"

"Yes," replied Paul. He told him the names of the films. "I'd like to see the one at the Strand," he added. They both flushed. They found it very difficult to be casual with each other.

"Would you like to come with me to-night?" asked Gary.

"Yes," replied Paul. It seemed to him that this

was the first time in his life that the things he had dreamed about were coming true. And he determined to cling to them, never, never to let them go.

"Excuse me, Gary," he said. "I'll have to ring up to tell them I won't be home until late."

He went to the telephone booth. It was Mrs. McKenzie who answered.

"Your father's just the same," she said.

"Will you ask my mother if she wants me to come home?" asked Paul, "or can I stay out until late?"

"Stay out as long as you like, Paul," said Mrs. McKenzie. "There's no use your coming back early to sit alone in the house."

"Thank you," said Paul.

"Are you going out with Bryan?" she asked.

"No," said Paul. He decided not to tell her about Gary. He did not want to tell anyone about Gary. But at least Mrs. McKenzie no longer seemed to mind his going out with Bryan, if he wanted to.

When he went back to the table, Gary said, "I hope you hadn't already arranged to go out with someone?"

"No," said Paul. "I was just making sure that no one at home needed me. Will you call for me at the shop about seven?"

"Yes," said Gary.

They lit cigarettes, and sat talking for a few minutes.

"Mr. Swallow told me that you had already got your degree in medicine," said Paul. "Is that right?"

"Yes," said Gary.

"Congratulations," said Paul. "What are you going to do now?"

"I've applied for a research fellowship," said Gary. "I'll know in a month or so whether or not I've got it."

"Does it mean very much to you?" asked Paul.

"Yes," said Gary, "I've been relying on it for the past two years."

"I'm sure that you'll get it," said Paul.

"Thank you, Paul," he said. "Are you going to go to university?"

"Yes," said Paul. "I'll probably do a degree in French and English."

"Then what will you do?" asked Gary.

"Get the most highly paid job that's going," said Paul.

Gary looked disappointed. "I'm sure that isn't your only ambition in life," he said.

"I've never had a purpose in life," said Paul. "I'm not like you, wanting to be a great doctor. I've never known what I wanted."

"Perhaps you do know," said Gary, "only you've dismissed it from your mind because you can't have it."

"That might be right," said Paul.

Gary insisted on paying for his tea, and Paul did not mind. He could pay for Gary at the pictures.

"I'll see you at seven," said Paul, as they came out of the café.

"Good-bye," said Gary.

He's a strange boy, thought Paul. I rarely know what he's thinking. He has many friends, yet he seems lonely. And beneath his pride, he's desperately shy. And I find it hard to talk to him, yet when I'm with him, I feel happy and secure.

II

Gary called at the shop before seven, but Mr. Swallow allowed Paul to leave early. As they walked down the road, both of them searched for something to say. They felt very awkward.

"The Promenade is crowded with girls looking for boy friends," Paul remarked.

"Do you go out with girls very often?" asked Gary.

"I used to," said Paul, "but not any more. They bore me."

"You didn't seem to be bored with the girl I saw you with the night before last," said Gary.

Paul flushed.

"I was tricked into taking her out," he said. "I won't do it again in a hurry."

From the amused look on his face, Paul thought that Gary did not believe him.

Just then they passed an amusement arcade.

"Let's go in here for a minute," said Gary.

The juke-box was blaring a rock 'n' roll tune, and teenagers were jiving self-consciously in the middle of the floor. The atmosphere was hot and exciting, and Paul wished that he were wearing the kind of clothes that would help him to fit with these people of his own age. He wished that he could jive.

Gary stood quietly by the juke-box, and presently he put in a coin. Paul watched the dancing, fascinated. Then Gary's record was played; it was slow and sentimental, and the dancing stopped immediately. Paul liked the record, but there were murmurs of discontent from the dancers, and some of them looked at Gary resentfully. He ignored them, and insisted on hearing the record to a close. Then he smiled at Paul, and they left the arcade.

"You're lucky you didn't start a rock 'n' roll riot," said Paul, laughing.

"I wanted to see what would happen," said Gary.

"Next time you're going to do anything like that,"

said Paul, "tell me, so that I can get ready to run."

"I promise," laughed Gary.

In the picture-house he sat with his knee pressed lightly against Paul's thigh, and Paul did not move. They smoked continually, and exchanged low remarks about the film, which was a glossy love story. They were warmly happy. After a time, Gary put his arm round the back of Paul's seat; Paul looked at him, and they smiled.

During the interval, Paul said, "That was a silly picture. The love affair was idealized, and there should have been a sad ending."

"I agree," said Gary. "Very few things in the world end happily."

"We're both cynics," said Paul.

"But it's true," said Gary. "Two people don't just fall in love, and that's the end of it. There are duties to their families to be considered, and their duty to their vocation. And besides, very few people are enough in love to spend the rest of their lives together. That only happens in books and films."

"I gather that you don't think very much of marriage," said Paul.

"No," said Gary. "I don't, unless two people are really so much in love, that they can't do without each other. You shouldn't marry for security, or because you're lonely, or you'll be more unhappy than ever."

When they came out of the cinema, Gary asked:
"Do you drink, Paul?"

"Yes," lied Paul.

"Will you come for a drink now?" he asked.

"I'd like to," said Paul.

The pub was crowded and noisy, but at last they found a table.

"I'd like a whisky, on the rocks," said Paul. He thought that was the right expression, for he had heard it used in American films. Gary brought two whiskies, and for a while they sat looking at each other over their glasses.

"To us," said Gary, raising his glass.

"No," said Paul. "To you. I hope you'll win your research fellowship."

"All right," said Gary, with an expression that Paul thought was ironic.

Paul thought that the whisky tasted lovely. He liked it much more than smoking. He soon finished it, and Gary asked, "Would you like another one?"

Paul would have liked another one, but he decided against it. "No," he replied. "I'd prefer a beer."

They stayed in the pub for over an hour, talking and smoking and drinking. Paul had one more beer, and cider, but Gary drank only whisky.

"Don't you think that you've had enough whisky, Gary?" asked Paul gently.

"No," said Gary, "I was drinking whisky when

I was younger than you are." He looked bitter. "It's great stuff. Makes you feel happy. I needed whisky and cigarettes, even when I was at school, for I worked like hell."

"But you have plenty of friends, and plenty of things that should amuse you," said Paul.

"I only keep my friends for a little while," said Gary, watching the liquid swill around the glass. "They bore me, usually. They're so stupid, and conventional, and they have no ambitions. And besides, very few of them liked having a friend who could come out so rarely. It just so happened that I met you during the one summer in my life when I didn't have to study. Otherwise you wouldn't have seen me for weeks after to-night. You'll come out with me to-morrow, won't you?"

"Yes," said Paul.

When they left the pub, Gary was not drunk, but he was happy. He put his arm round Paul's shoulder to steady himself, and he kept it there, all the way home. They made their way along the promenade, and up past Mr. Swallow's shop. It was closed, and there was no light in any of the windows of his house. He must be in bed for want of anything better to do, thought Paul.

"I'm going to come home with you," said Gary.

"No, you're not," said Paul hastily. "You're going to go straight home to bed."

Gary tried to open his eyes a little wider. "Well, then," he said, "I'm going to kiss you good night."

"Don't be disgusting," said Paul. "You're drunker . . . more drunk . . . no, drunker . . ."

While he struggled for the right comparative, Gary threw up his arms, and laughed uproariously. Then he quietened, and looked at Paul seriously. He looked like a child who had been disappointed. "But I want to kiss you," he said.

"Do you know what you are?" asked Paul.

"I know what I am as regards you," said Gary.

"Good night," said Paul. "I'll see you to-morrow."

III

When Paul arrived home, his mother was waiting in the kitchen. She had obviously recovered from the shock of Mr. Anderson's collapse.

"You're very late," she said, "seeing that your father is lying upstairs dying."

"Is he any worse?" asked Paul.

"No," she admitted.

"Well then," said Paul, "the doctor told you it

might be weeks before father died. There doesn't seem to be much point in my staying in every night."

"Is that an indication of how much you loved him?" she asked.

"Perhaps it is," replied Paul, "but at least I'm not afraid to admit it. Have you spoken to Father to-day?"

"Yes," she replied.

"What did you say to him?" asked Paul.

"What could I say to him? I told him to lie quietly, and that there was a good chance of his getting better, and that I was going to bring the minister to see him."

"God!" exclaimed Paul, "Father knows as well as we do that he's going to die, and the last person on earth that he wants to see is a minister. He doesn't give a damn for religion."

"How can you talk like that?" asked Mrs. Anderson. "What else could I say to him?"

"You could have apologized," suggested Paul.

She was amazed. "Apologized?" she asked. "What had I to apologize for?"

"For making his life a hell for the past few years," said Paul.

"I don't know what you're talking about," she said coldly. "If you're going to argue with me, I'll go up to my room. You have some of the stupidest ideas I've ever heard of. I did all I could for your father. I tried to make him happy."

"You stupid bitch," shouted Paul. "Do you really believe that, or can you not face up to the truth? Aren't you ashamed of the way you treated Father? In front of Mrs. McKenzie and Bryan, you apologized for his behaviour, and you treated him like a child who had no more sense."

Mrs. Anderson looked white and shocked.

"How dare you?" she asked. "What right have you to shout at me when you yourself treated your father so badly. Have you been out with Bryan to-night? Was it Bryan who put these notions into your head?"

"No," replied Paul. "I was out with someone else, someone whom you don't know."

"Well you're not going out with him again until I meet him," she said.

"You won't meet him," said Paul, "and I'm going out with him to-morrow night. I used to pity you, but now I'm beginning to wonder just how hard and calculating you are. I'm going to bed, and if you try to do anything to stop me going out to-morrow night, I'm leaving home, and you can go to hell."

Paul knew that Gary was exactly the sort of friend his mother had always wanted for him, the kind of whom she could boast to Mrs. McKenzie.

When Paul went upstairs, Mrs. McKenzie was sitting by his father's bed.

"He's unconscious again," she said. "Did you have a nice time?"

"Yes, I had a very nice time," he said.

"I'm glad," said Mrs. McKenzie. "Paul, I want you to know that I don't mind your going out with Bryan. He's been lonely lately and he needs a friend."

"I'm sorry," said Paul, "but I won't be going out with Bryan again. We agreed not to. We only argue and fight."

"I see," said Mrs. McKenzie. "If that's the way you feel there's nothing more to be said."

She thought Paul had deserted Bryan for another friend. In a way it was quite true.

PART TWO

CHAPTER VIII

I

PAUL thought that the summer was going to go on for ever. The hot blue days followed each other, until he forgot about the autumn and the winter that were coming. He was happier than he had ever been before, and the heat clouded his mind, and he seldom thought about the future.

Other people were rather jealous of him. He saw little of Bryan, for he never came to the house. Mrs. McKenzie treated him a little coldly, for she resented the fact that Paul was so happy, while Bryan was lonely. And Mrs. Anderson resented the fact that Paul refused to remain at home and wait quietly for his father's death. Mr. Anderson gradually became worse, but he lived for a month after the night he collapsed. During the last fortnight he could hardly speak or move, and he had to be fed through a tube. Mrs. McKenzie remained at the house until he died, but although Mrs. Anderson paid her, she grew more impatient every day.

There was something in his mother's attitude

towards him that Paul could not define. The nearest he could get to it was that she was apprehensive. But he could think of no reason. She knew that her husband was going to die, and by now she must have become used to it. She also knew that Paul had promised to go to university, and he meant to keep his promise, although he did not want to. He thought that perhaps she dreaded the time of the funeral, when the house would be crowded with insincere mourners. But Paul did not think about his mother very much.

He was on good terms with Mr. Swallow. They often sat in the shop and had long arguments, which had very little point, for Mr. Swallow had made up his mind about most things a long time ago, and he had no intention of changing it now. He professed to be a firm believer in Christ, although he never went to church.

"Then you believe in life after death?" asked Paul.

"Of course," said Mr. Swallow. "Otherwise life would have no purpose."

"Some people find the purpose of life in their vocation," said Paul. "My best friend says that the thing in life that matters most to him is medicine. He would give up everything else for it, even though it doesn't give him happiness. But I certainly don't believe in life after death. There is only peace, and I'd prefer that to being an angel."

"Then what happens to all the people who have been wicked in this life?" asked Mr. Swallow. "Aren't they punished?"

"No," replied Paul, "for wickedness is relative. No one can really say what is right and what is wrong."

"You'd better watch out," said Mr. Swallow. "There was once a man who talked exactly the way you do, and one day he was sitting on the wall by the sea, when he had a heart attack, and he died straight off."

"Thank you for being so reassuring," said Paul drily.

II

Paul and Gary loved each other, although Gary never mentioned it after the night when he drank too much whisky. They went out with each other almost every night, and spent the whole of each Saturday and Sunday together. Not once during the summer did it rain when they were out together.

They made trips into the surrounding countryside in Gary's car. Gary drove it along the deserted roads at high speeds, and at the times when it reached a hundred Paul felt very near to . . . but he could not name this inexpressible feeling of sadness and ecstasy. Gary tried to teach him to drive, but he very soon lost patience, and they nearly had an argument over it. Then Gary started laughing, and they were as happy as before. But there was still a solemnness between them, as if they had thought a great deal about each other, and they did not want to spoil their relationship by saying stupid things. And Paul often noticed that Gary looked sad, when he should have been happy.

On their trips into the country they took sandwiches, cigarettes and beer, sometimes whisky, and Gary parked the car on a lonely road, near a deserted field. There they spent the rest of the day, lying in the sun and talking quietly, or perhaps listening to music on the portable radio.

One Sunday morning at the end of July, as they were driving out of the town, Gary said, "Paul, you remember you said that someday you'd tell me why you stopped going to church? Will you tell me now?"

"Why do you want to know?" asked Paul.

"I was just thinking that I haven't been to church since I met you," said Gary.

"I'm a bad influence on you," laughed Paul.

"Tell me, Paul."

"All right. When I was thirteen I was converted at a watch-night service. The idea of being converted appealed to me, and I was feeling bad at the time, for Bryan was at boarding school, and I was rather lonely. I was converted, and for a few months I was a very ardent Christian, thinking that the greatest joy in life was to help someone else see the light, and so on. I went to church twice on Sunday, and I took Communion. I went to a Church Society, a young people's meeting, and I made friends, but they weren't the sort of friends I wanted. And I found that although they were supposed to be Christians, they took their religion less seriously than I did. Then at school the hear-no-evil attitude didn't exactly make you very popular.

"Bryan came back from boarding school, and I began going to the pictures, and smoking a little. At the beginning, I thought those things were terrible sins. Then I began reading some books, and I started thinking. Who can prove that there is a God? Is it likely that a God of Love would send people to hell because they have been wicked? And isn't it a lot of nonsense that God should send His Son down to atone for our sins? And how did God come into being? If He wanted us to understand Him why didn't He give us more powerful minds? And religion is purely a local affair. If you're born in one country you're a Buddhist, if you're born in another you're a Christian. Yet every member of a religion thinks that his religion is the right one. How can I be sure that Christianity is the right religion, just because I was born in Britain?

"Finally, I decided that Jesus Christ must have been a rather kind man, but a religious fanatic, obsessed by the idea that he was the Son of God. So gradually I gave up religion, and stopped going to church."

Gary remained silent for a moment, then he asked, "What do you believe in, Paul?"

"I don't think I believe in anything," he said.

"Do you not perhaps believe in Humanism?" asked Gary.

"In a way," replied Paul, "but after all, you yourself are human, and if you believe that your mission is to help the human race, you might as well look after yourself first and foremost."

Gary smiled. "I agree with everything you said about religion," he said.

Paul was surprised. "Then why do you go to church?" he asked.

"It's hard to explain what I believe," said Gary. "I believe in good and evil, and I suppose that they are personified by God and the Devil. I don't believe that if you wallow in sin you won't enjoy it, but in the long run it's bad, both for yourself and the rest of the human race. That's partly why I want to be a doctor. I could serve other people. The other reason is personal glory. I want to be famous."

"Do you believe that good will finally overcome evil?" asked Paul.

"No," said Gary. "Good will never win, for the battle will continue as long as there are human beings in existence."

"Yours is a very cold faith," said Paul. "It isn't what I would want. I want a faith that will give me security, and love."

"You can't have a faith like that," said Gary, "unless you believe in a personal God."

"But whom do you worship in church," asked Paul, "if you don't believe in God?"

"Sometimes I'm able to convince myself that there is someone like God," said Gary. "Otherwise, I suppose I worship good."

"I think that's what I believe, too," said Paul, "only I'm not brave enough to accept it. It gives one a purpose in life—to be good—but there is no reward of love or security. There are times when I hate people who call themselves Christians. They use the Church as a means of social intercourse, and they push religion into the background. They blind themselves to the poverty in the world, and the sickness and the misery. I don't think I could ever be permanently happy when I knew that these things existed, and most fortunate people just ignore them.

Life is a tragedy, Gary. What else could it be? It's lonely and cruel and futile."

"But it's also very short," said Gary, half-smiling. "And when we die, we endure no more misery. We get peace at last. Life's really a comedy: it has a happy ending."

"Then people are fools," said Paul. "They delude themselves into thinking that tomorrow will be better, when they could end their lives so quickly. Gary, I wish that I had something to devote my life to, like you have."

"You wouldn't be any happier," said Gary. "Sometimes you would be miserable. And besides, you can't just adopt something because you want to devote your life to a vocation. Perhaps you will find a person to love."

They were suddenly silent. Paul loved Gary, so that should give him a purpose in life, but people said that kind of love was wrong.

Gary parked the car by a field. There were horses at one end, and at the other there was a river, and a willow tree.

Paul and Gary lay in the sun, and for a while it seemed that they were contented. Suddenly Gary turned on his side, and lay stretched out, gazing at Paul.

"What are the things you like doing most in the world?" he asked.

Paul flushed. "They're very silly things," he stammered.

"Tell me about them," said Gary.

"Well," said Paul, "I like whisky, and cigarettes, and driving at high speeds. I like watching the sea in winter, when the water is calm and grey, and the mountains across the sea are hidden by mist. I like woods in winter, when the trees are bare and dark, and there is snow. I like to sit by a blazing fire, and read a book, when there's a storm blowing outside." He gestured awkwardly. "They're only silly things," he said.

When Gary did not reply, he went on, "I like the last few moments in bed in the morning. And lying in the sun on a hot summer day."

"With me?" asked Gary, as though that was what he had been waiting for.

"Yes, of course," said Paul. He watched Gary carefully. His hair caught the sunlight, and his eyes were screwed up against the sun. The skin on his face glowed in the warmth, and around his eyes it was dark, as if he usually wore glasses, and he had just then taken them off.

"Paul," he said, looking at the ground, "I love you very much."

Paul suddenly felt sick. The ground beneath him seemed to take a sudden leap. He closed his eyes, to relieve his emotion. He felt Gary's arm around his shoulder, and Gary's body pressed tightly against his.

Gary said, "Paul, I love you, I love you."

Paul opened his eyes, and saw Gary's face inches away. For a moment he watched the tenderness, and let Gary lie with him. Then suddenly he wriggled away, and stood up.

"It's wrong," he shouted. Gary stood up and came towards him.

"Go away," cried Paul. "How can you talk about dedicating your life to good when you want to do this with me."

"My making love to you isn't bad," said Gary.

"I know it isn't," said Paul, "but that isn't what other people think. Comedians make filthy jokes about this sort of thing, and they do ugly caricatures of people with a B.B.C. announcer's accent."

"But I love you Paul," said Gary. "We're not those sort of people."

"Then what are we?" asked Paul.

"Have you ever met a homosexual?" asked Gary. "Do you know what homosexuality is? It's wanting to fiddle with every little boy you see. It's standing on the pier waiting for the next boatload of sailors to come in. It's giving women an inferiority complex. It's standing taking peeks in a man's toilet. I'm not like that, Paul. I love you, I love you."

"Perhaps you're not like that now," said Paul,

"but perhaps someday you will be if you go on like this."

Gary hit him across the mouth.

"I'm sorry," cried Paul. "Don't you see what I mean? I love you, too, but people say that it's evil. It makes you an outcast from society. People would never have you as a doctor if they thought you were having a love affair with another man."

Gary turned away, and Paul looked at him helplessly.

"We'd better go," said Gary.

They returned to the car in silence. As they drove home, Gary stared straight in front of him. Paul wanted with all his heart to comfort him, but he was sick with fright. Frightened of his own emotions, and what the future might bring.

"When will you know if you've won the research fellowship?" asked Paul.

"Soon," replied Gary. His mouth twitched, and he looked at Paul. "I'm not angry with you," he said, "but we had better not go out with each other again, Paul."

Paul did not reply. When they reached the house, and Paul was getting out of the car, Gary said, "I'm sorry, Paul. This summer was wonderful." Then abruptly, he backed the car, and drove away.

I'll see him every day, thought Paul, even though I never speak to him.

He went into the house. Three more weeks and the summer will have ended. But I'll see Gary again. He won't just disappear from the world when the summer ends. He'll be living here, although he may have his fellowship in a hospital in the city.

But I should have known this would happen. This is the way it's always been. When I had something I lost it, every time. And people say that everything's for the best, and someday God will make it right again.

Paul went up to his room, and closed the door. He stared at himself in the mirror. Beneath his tan he was very pale. His eyes were bloodshot from cigarette smoke, and his lips were dry. Suddenly he picked up a book and threw it at the mirror. It cracked in two, and the tiny splinters tumbled down on to the book which had fallen on the floor. They caught the sunlight, and formed a bright crazy pattern.

"I won't believe in a bloody, blasted, damned maniac God!" shouted Paul. "What have I ever had to give me faith in Him? I'm a fool, but at least I have a little spirit, and while I keep that, I'll fight for all I'm worth."

The tears were running down his face, and his body was shocked and trembling. He threw himself on the bed, and buried his head in the pillow. He felt complete horror and loathing of life, yet the thing that never occurred to him was to end it. There was a frantic sickness in the world, and in Paul himself, and he was powerless to conquer it, and all his efforts made him appear more puny.

This was the moment for which the years had been preparing him. They had made him poor, and sick and stupid. He had never known what he wanted, and still he did not know. He wanted to be back with Gary, and he wanted to love Gary. But he was frightened of all the things that might happen. He was too sensitive to ignore the world, he could not bear the thought of being an outcast.

He heard the door open, and hastily he tried to wipe away his tears. His mother stood at the door for a moment, and asked, "Is there something wrong, Paul?" Then she rushed over to the bed. "What's wrong, Paul? What are you crying for?"

He shook her hand from his shoulder. "Go away and leave me alone," he said, and stood up, wiping his face with his hands and blowing his nose.

Mrs. Anderson noticed the mirror for the first time. "What happened, Paul?" she asked.

"I'll pay for it," shouted Paul. "Leave me alone."

"You're not in any trouble, are you?" she asked.

"Trust you to think of that," he said. "I'm not in any trouble. It's just that I suddenly became tired of the summer and everything and everybody and—

well; I'm growing up, so I suppose that has something to do with it."

"Very well," she said. "I'll go. I'm sorry you won't tell me what's wrong. You'd better clean up the pieces of glass."

"I'll be all right, Mother," said Paul.

When she had gone he stood at the window, and let the breeze from the sea cool his face.

CHAPTER IX

I

PAUL spent the next few days waiting for teatime, when he knew that he would see Gary leaving the factory. But when Gary came out he headed straight for home, without a glance across at the shop. Time was a nightmare for Paul. He tried to read while he was at the shop, but he could not concentrate for more than a few minutes, and then old thoughts came crowding back to him, and he was lying in a green summer field, or standing on the rocks, watching ships on the horizon. He could not see a way out of the tiny room, filled with conflicting emotions and desires, hopes and dreams, fear and love, in which he was imprisoned.

At night he went to the pictures, but he could not sit still, and when the lights went up, he felt that everyone glanced at him, noticing that he was alone, and then forgetting him. The films seemed to be long and dreary, and he usually left the cinema before they ended. Then on the crowded promenade, his shyness and self-consciousness returned, and he went up side-streets to avoid seeing groups of people of his own age. One night, he tried staying at home, but it was hellish. He sat in his room, fidgeting with a cigarette and a book, and listening to the radio. Restlessly, he wandered into his father's room, but Mr. Anderson was unconscious. Downstairs Mrs. McKenzie was talking to his mother, and they ignored him. He thought of ringing up Robin Forrest, but then he knew that he could not bear anyone's company. Each day, he knew that to-morrow would be no better.

II

Late one night, Mr. Anderson died. At one o'clock, Paul was wakened by Mrs. McKenzie. "Come quickly," she said. "Your father's dying."

The words had little effect on Paul. He felt no sorrow. He responded to what seemed the call of duty towards the man who was his father, although to Paul he was a stranger. When he went into the bedroom, he saw that his father's eyes were open. Mrs. Anderson was sitting at the bottom of the bed, with a dazed expression on her face, and Mrs. McKenzie hovered in the background. Paul came close to his father, and Mr. Anderson's eyes flickered with light for a moment.

"Paul," he whispered, "when I die, go away from here." His voice tailed off. His eyes closed. He lived for another hour, and when he died, he looked peaceful and happy.

The atmosphere of a house where a person had died had an effect on Paul. His movements were still aimless, but the torment left him, and seemed to be replaced by resignation.

He went to Mr. Swallow's, and got two days off work. He sent off all the telegrams, and called at the undertaker's. He bought food for the meal to be served after the funeral, and received callers at the house. He bought a black suit for the funeral. It was something that he had never possessed before, and he looked well in it, for he was pale and serious-looking.

The funeral took place in the late afternoon, and it was another beautiful day. The minister who took charge of the service had only seen Mr. Anderson a few times during his life, but he used to know Paul well. His name was the Rev. Crawford. He was well fed, with a small brain and large paunch. He was ambitious, and he did not dwell too long on religion. Paul sensed the core of worldliness in him, and despised him for it, although he knew that it was right that he should be worldly.

The cemetery was on a hill, and as the group of people, most of whom Paul had never seen before, gathered round the grave, Paul thought, "My father loved me." That meant something, but he did not know what it was. He thought, "When you're dying life must seem very simple. My father told me to leave my mother, and do whatever I wanted. But where would I go, and what would I do. It isn't as easy as that. And I don't care much any more. If I got to university in the city, that's probably where Gary will be working, and we might travel on the same train."

The coffin was lowered into the grave, and as Rev. Crawford spoke insincerely, Bryan whispered in Paul's ear, "I wish this was over, so that we could get home and have a feed."

Paul respected Bryan for that remark, for he knew that the other mourners were thinking exactly the same thing, although they would not have admitted it.

Bryan and Paul were leaving the cemetery, together, in a hurry to get a taxi before they were all filled, when Rev. Crawford stopped them.

"Paul, I hope I shall be seeing more of you in church now," he said.

"Why?" asked Paul coldly. The Rev. Crawford considered that. He never knew what to do when someone was hostile to him, but somehow he had to end the conversation, so he said doubtfully, "It was your father's illness that was keeping you from church, wasn't it?"

"No," replied Paul, "I just didn't want to go. I hate church."

The Rev. Crawford's wonderfully calm face gave no indication of what he was thinking.

"I'll have a talk with you again," he said hastily, and walked away gracefully.

"Good for you," said Bryan.

"I'm outside the pale for ever, now," said Paul.

"And I bet you're glad," said Bryan. "Soon I shall be outside it too."

They ran for a taxi. When they were inside Paul slammed the door and told the driver to take them home without waiting for anyone else.

Then he turned to Bryan and asked, "When are you leaving home?"

"In a couple of weeks," said Bryan. "When I finish my work at the nursery."

"I wish I could come with you," said Paul.

"Why don't you?" asked Bryan.

"I can't leave my mother. Besides, when it came to the point I might not want to leave—not any more. University will probably be as good as anything I could find for myself."

Bryan said, "You've been going around with John Knight this summer, haven't you, Paul?"

"Yes," said Paul, "but I won't be going out with him again."

"Did you have a row?" asked Bryan.

"No," said Paul, "we just ended it. Gary—John is so much older than I am."

"He's a very nice person," said Bryan.

"Do you know him?" asked Paul.

"No," said Bryan. "I've just seen him in church."

"What did you do during the summer?" asked Paul.

Bryan flushed. "Nothing very much," he replied. "I've been saving my pay, so I couldn't spend money. I'll need it all when I leave home."

Paul hesitated, then he said, "Bryan, I hope you didn't mind my spending the summer with John. It's just that, well, you know the way we argued and fought when we were together. Your mother was upset, because you had no one to go out with."

"I understand," said Bryan. He changed the subject. "Have you seen Rosemary lately?"

"No," said Paul. "I'd forgotten all about her."

"You've got a very bad memory," said Bryan drily. "A month ago you were very upset because she had seduced you. You went around with your nose in the air, as though you were above such things as sex. All I can say is that you're a lucky bugger. I wish *I* could find someone with whom I could lose my bloody virginity."

138

I do forget things easily, thought Paul, but I shall never forget Gary. It's strange. I pretend to be miserable, but I really enjoy my misery. I *want* to remember Gary, and be sad, always.

When they arrived home, and went into the sitting-room, it was already crowded. Mrs. McKenzie was serving tea, and Mrs. Anderson was talking animatedly with a long-lost acquaintance. Paul greeted a few relations hastily, and then collecting two cups of tea and some food, he led Bryan up to his room.

They ate in silence. Then Paul said, "If you like you can smoke a cigar. I don't mind. I shall have more freedom now. My mother's depending on me to go to university, and she knows that if she says very much, I'll just leave her."

"What happened to the mirror?" asked Bryan.

"I broke it when I was in a bad temper," said Paul.

"Gosh," said Bryan, "you're branching out."

"I've got something else to show you," said Paul. He rolled back the mattress on his bed, and took out a bottle of whisky. Bryan's eyes widened. "Are you going to drink that?" he asked.

"*We* are going to drink it," replied Paul. He poured some out into a glass, and held it out to Bryan. Bryan took it nervously. Paul held up his own glass.

"To you," he said dramatically. "May your future be as happy as mine will be unhappy."

Bryan laughed. "Stop acting," he said. "You're getting as bad as Rosemary."

He swallowed a little whisky. "Ugh!" he groaned, and coughed violently.

"Watch!" said Paul, and he gulped down a glassful. Then he repeated the performance. After that there was no whisky left.

"I wish I'd bought half a dozen bottles," said Paul. "Then I could have got drunk and gone down into the drawing-room and shocked everyone. Gary got drunk once."

"Who's Gary?" asked Bryan.

"Somebody," said Paul.

"You've changed, Paul," said Bryan.

"Of course I've changed," said Paul. "I've discovered that I can be as rude and violent as I like, and no one will think any worse of me. From now on I'm going to do just as I like." He paused, and looked sad. "Only," he added, "when I haven't had any whisky to drink, I'm quiet and shy again."

"You're just a crazy mixed-up kid," laughed Bryan. "Why don't you get a Teddy-boy outfit and learn to rock 'n' roll?"

"Very funny," said Paul sarcastically.

"The trouble with you," said Bryan, "is that you don't know what you want. *I* want to go my own sweet way, without any interference from my mother."

"So do I," interrupted Paul.

"Yes," said Bryan, "but your own sweet way doesn't make you happy."

"That isn't my fault," said Paul. "Life's like that. If you have one thing you have to do without another. I'm not really selfish. I've seldom had anything I really wanted, and when I did get it for a while, it was taken away again."

"I was only joking," said Bryan. "Do you wish that you were adopted too?" Paul looked at him in amazement, but he saw that there was no need for pretence. Bryan was looking at him quite frankly.

"Yes," said Paul, "I do wish that I was adopted; then I should have no reason to blame my mother for not loving me."

"Do you mean that I have no right to pity myself?" asked Bryan.

"No," said Paul. "But I can understand Mrs. McKenzie's wanting to make the best of you. She feels that you owe her something—more than if you had been one of her own children."

"Do you think I'm right to run away?"

"Yes, but I'm sorry for Mrs. McKenzie. She hasn't been very friendly with me lately, because I didn't go out with you during the summer, but she has been very kind to my mother; kinder than my mother deserved."

He went to the window. "Look," he said, "they're beginning to leave at last."

"I'd better go too," said Bryan. "I have to make my father's tea."

"Come into the shop and see me sometime before you leave home," said Paul.

"I will," said Bryan. "And don't drink too much whisky."

When Bryan had gone, Paul thought: he's quite happy, he accepts things more easily than I do. But why should anyone have to make do with second best, while other people get the best?

He went downstairs about an hour later. Everyone had gone, and his mother was sitting alone in the kitchen.

"Where's Mrs. McKenzie?" asked Paul.

"She left with Bryan," said Mrs. Anderson. "She wasn't needed any longer."

Paul wandered about the room aimlessly, until his mother said, "Come and sit down, Paul. I have something to tell you."

He sat down obediently. He hoped that he was going to hear something interesting.

"Paul, did you know that after your father died, his pension would stop, and I wouldn't get any money from the firm for which he used to work?"

"No," said Paul. "Surely that doesn't mean that

all you have now is the money you were saving for me to go to university?"

"That's exactly what I do mean," she said.

"Then I shall have to get a job," said Paul.

"No," said his mother firmly. "No matter what else happens, you're going to university. I shall get a job, you can work during the vacation, and anyhow, you'll probably get a scholarship on the results of your examination."

"I won't," said Paul.

"From now on we're going to have to plan carefully," said his mother. "I may tell you, Paul, that at first I was glad that all the trouble with your father was going to end, but now I wish that he had at least lived until you had your degree."

Paul thought that in her illogical heart she was probably blaming her husband for dying at such an awkward time.

"What kind of work will you do?" he asked.

"Private nursing," his mother replied at once. Obviously she had already planned the details of her new position in life.

"It doesn't take you long to get used to your new circumstances, does it, Mother?" he asked.

"No," she replied. "That's what's wrong with you, Paul. You're not resourceful enough."

"I don't think we'll have enough money," said Paul.

"Of course we will," said Mrs. Anderson. "We'll manage somehow, so don't be getting any idea into your head about taking a permanent job. How much money have you saved from your job at Mr. Swallow's?"

"About ten pounds," replied Paul.

"It could have been more," she said, "but at least it will buy your books. We'll talk about it again when you get your results. When do they come out?"

"In about a fortnight," said Paul.

As he went up to bed he realized that the fact that she would have so little money made very little difference to his mother. In a way, he envied her. He wished that he was capable of making a decision, and never varying from it, whatever happened. He wished that he had a will like Gary's. Gary had decided to become a doctor, and nothing in the world would stop him. Paul remembered his own restless attempts to settle down with a book when he was studying for his examination, and he knew that at university it would be the same. Before he could work hard at a thing, he had to enjoy doing it, no matter what the reward might be.

CHAPTER X

I

PAUL went back to work in Mr. Swallow's next morning. Mr. Swallow was embarrassed, and Paul sympathized with him. He would not have known what to say if he had been in Mr. Swallow's position.

"How is your mother, Paul?" he asked.

"She's all right," said Paul, "though she still hasn't got over the shock." That was surprising, for Mrs. Anderson had known for a month that her husband was going to die, but Paul had to say something.

Mr. Swallow retired to the back of the shop, and Paul settled down with a book.

A customer came in. Paul looked up. It was Gary.

"I'm sorry, Paul," he said. "I came into the shop yesterday to see you, and Mr. Swallow told me about your father. I'm sorry."

Paul looked at him. On no one else's face had he ever seen such love and sympathy. Behind them, there was sadness, as there had always been, but now it was more noticeable.

He hesitated. "Paul," he said, "I have something to tell you. Can I pick you up in the car after work?"

"Of course," said Paul.

Gary parked the car in a lane, and then leaned back in his seat. Paul turned his head and watched him silently. Outside the car, the sun was setting, and the lane was shaded, but dappled with brilliant patches of light. The heat of the summer and the absence of rain had dried the leaves of the trees, so that some of them were already falling, while others hung crisply to the branches. Soon it would be early autumn, the sad time of the year that Paul loved most. This year it was premature, for part of the summer had still to run its course. But soon, with September, the real autumn would begin.

Paul knew that he should be happy, for he was with Gary again, but he sensed Gary's sadness.

Gary said, "I'm so sorry about your father. I suppose his death was sudden?"

"No," said Paul. "I knew all summer that he was going to die."

Gary looked at him. "Is that why you looked so sad?" he asked.

"No," said Paul. "I didn't know that I looked sad. I thought you were the sad one."

"You didn't love your father, did you?" asked Gary.

"No," said Paul. "But he loved me."

"I thought that," said Gary. "My father died when I was ten years old, and I loved him very much. I haven't stopped missing him yet. Paul, I want to tell you something."

Paul waited. The inside of the car was warm, and there were few sounds from the world outside. Paul felt so near to Gary, yet both of them were making sure that no part of their bodies touched.

"I've won my research fellowship," said Gary.

"I'm so glad," said Paul. "I knew you'd win it. Is it in a hospital in the city?"

"No," said Gary.

"Then where is it?"

"Southern Rhodesia."

The words hit Paul softly, like a soundless blow on a silk cushion. They left an emptiness, where there had never been anything. Gary sat looking through the windscreen at the trees, numb with tenderness and compassion, while Paul remained motionless, shocked into silence.

"When do you leave?" he asked.

"Monday week."

"How long will you be gone?"

"Three years," said Gary, "unless I can afford to pay my passage home for holidays, and I can't do that."

"I don't know what to say or do," said Paul.

"I understand," said Gary. He reached out and took Paul's hand.

"I know you understand," said Paul. Gary's hand was strong and warm. He clasped it tightly.

"Paul," said Gary, "we have a week left. Let's spend it together and have the time of our lives. I'm giving up my job to-morrow; you could do the same."

"I'll tell Mr. Swallow in the morning," said Paul, without hesitation. He sat still for a moment, then he said, "Gary, I don't care if loving you is wrong. It can't be, and even if it is, I don't care any more. If I let you go now, without telling you, I should regret it for the rest of my life."

He put his arms round Gary's neck, then leaned his head on his shoulder. He heard and felt Gary sigh, and he said, "Strangely enough, I think this makes me more manly. This is the first time in my life when I've made a decision that needed courage. I'm sure you've been brave all your life."

11

Next morning, Paul told Mr. Swallow that he was leaving the shop. "I want to get some fresh air and sunshine before the summer ends completely," he said.

"Do you want to leave to-day?" asked Mr. Swallow.

"Yes," said Paul. "Will you be able to manage the shop by yourself?"

"Yes," said Mr. Swallow, "most of the summer business has gone."

Paul wondered just how deserted the shop was in the winter. For a moment he was conscience-stricken. He knew that Mr. Swallow had been grateful for his company in the past weeks.

"Are you sure you'll be able to manage?" he asked.

"Yes."

Paul sighed. "Very well," he said.

In his pay-packet that night there was an extra pound.

"It's too much," said Paul. "I'm sure you can't afford to give pound notes away."

"You can be sure I don't do it very often, Paul," said Mr. Swallow drily.

"I'll come in and see you often," said Paul, "and perhaps, if you want me to, I could come again next summer.

"We'll see," he said. "God knows where we'll all be next summer."

He's lonely, he needs someone, thought Paul, but

there's nothing I can do about it. An extra week or so of my working in the shop wouldn't do much good. And he's getting old. Older people don't mind loneliness so much. They've had their happiness.

III

On the last Sunday, they drove to a beach miles round the coast. Gary parked the car on the road above, and they had to scramble down a bank and through woods before they came to the beach. The sea was blue and the day was cloudless, but when they undressed and lay on the sand, Gary said, "It's colder to-day. That's the first time I've noticed it."

"The summer's ending," said Paul. "When you've gone, I shall often come to this beach, and all the other places we went to together. Only then it will be winter, and the sea will be rough, and the seaweed will be tossed high up on the beach."

"What are you going to do when I leave?" asked Gary.

"Go to university," said Paul. "I'll probably teach, if I manage to get my degree."

"Of course you'll get a degree," said Gary, "and you'll get a good one. By the time you do that, I shall probably have discovered a miraculous cure for cancer, or something."

"Or something," said Paul. "What will it be like in Southern Rhodesia?"

"Well," said Gary, "the hospital will be very modern, for it was set up by an American fund. The staff is African, but the more important people are whites. I shall be doing junior research work in tropical diseases, but that means that I shall probably be playing second fiddle to some famous doctor. At least it'll be experience."

"When you talk like that," said Paul, "I feel happy, because you're going to be very happy."

"You have impatient years before you, Paul," said Gary. "When I was at university, I was almost too busy dreaming to do any work. But if you don't work, you don't get the rewards."

"No," said Paul, "but then, I shouldn't regard working in a school as a reward."

"Then perhaps you won't be a teacher," said Gary. "Perhaps by then you'll have found the job in life that really interests you."

"Where will you go when your fellowship time is up," asked Paul.

"It depends," said Gary. "If I can save up enough money, I shall do a year of research on my own. If

I can't manage that, then I shall try for some other fellowship. I shall certainly never settle down to being an ordinary little doctor."

"Of course you won't," said Paul. "Someday, when you're very famous, and you will be, never doubt that, I shall write to you and ask you if you remember a boy called Paul Anderson. And you'll say, 'Oh, yes, he used to have a schoolboy crush on me'."

"No," said Gary violently. "You must never think that. You're too mature to have a schoolboy's crush on anyone, and I'm certainly too old."

"I know, I know," said Paul, "but I was only making that up to hear what you would say. Let's go for a swim."

Without waiting for a reply, he sprang up from the sand, and raced down to the sea. He plunged into the water, and swam strongly out to sea. Only when he turned to lie on his back did he realize that Gary had not followed him. He looked back towards the beach, and saw that Gary was wading in shallow water. Paul waved, to tell Gary to come to him, but Gary shook his head. Finally, Paul swam back to him. "What's wrong?" he asked.

Gary flushed. "I can't swim," he admitted.

Paul grinned. "I'm sorry," he said. "I took it for granted that you could swim, you're so good at other sports."

"The only games I play are rugby and hockey," said Gary.

"Would you like me to teach you how to swim?" asked Paul.

"No," said Gary, "let's go and lie on the sand again."

"All right," said Paul. "I don't mind. The water was colder than usual anyhow."

For some reason he was pleased that Gary could not swim, and he smiled when he thought of how embarrassed he had been when he had to admit it.

They lay down on the sand again, Gary's strong, pale-skinned body beside Paul's thin, brown one. Paul had the old feeling of warmth and protection from all that people could do to him. It was the same if his sleeve touched Gary's, or if he touched the warmth of a seat where Gary had been sitting. It was the same feeling that he had had in church on a winter's night, years ago. It had always been like this, really, although he had not realized it.

Gary asked, "Whom will you have for friends when I'm gone?"

"I don't know," said Paul. "Bryan McKenzie is leaving home, Robin Forrest bores me. So do they all, for that matter."

"You won't stay alone all the time, will you?" asked Gary.

"I shall probably make friends at university, and

join different societies," said Paul. "Do you know, I think I'll make a resolution to work really hard. I won't be restless any more. You've cured me of that. I'll work very hard, and get a first-class degree, then I'll do an advanced degree, and I shall probably end up as the Dean of a faculty in a famous university. Then I'll be as famous as you some day."

Gary laughed. "You're a little fool, Paul," he said. "You know as well as I do that you'll never work hard at any dull academic subject. Why don't you write novels? You seem just the type."

"What is the type?" asked Paul.

"Well," said Gary, "if you're going to write novels, real novels, you have to be a rather sad person, and you have to be sensitive. Then it's rather an advantage to have had an unhappy love affair, and the more unconventional it was, the better. So you seem to have all the qualifications."

Paul looked at him. Gary was smiling gently. "As well as that," he added, "you take everything so seriously. That would be another advantage."

Paul turned away. He heard Gary say, "I shall write to you every week, and tell you all the news, and you'll see that three years will pass quickly."

"Do you really believe that it's as simple as that?" asked Paul.

"Of course it is," said Gary. "Why shouldn't it be?"

Paul looked at him again. "Gary," he said, "I know I'm much younger than you are, but you are incredibly naïve. If you come home in three years, we won't just be able to pick up where we left off. You'll be a man by then, an adult, while I shall be your age. Both of us will have changed so much."

"I know, Paul," said Gary. "But I didn't think you knew, and I wanted to let you be happy for a while longer. I've known since the beginning of the summer that it was going to end soon. We can't carry it on through life, no matter how sad we are. But Paul, I shall always remember it. It's the happiest time I've ever known."

"It was part of growing up, wasn't it?" asked Paul.

They stayed out in the car all night. Then, in the morning, as Paul left him, Gary said, "God bless you, Paul. Good luck . . . always."

That's a strange thing to say, thought Paul, numbly : Gary doesn't believe in God.

He went into the house and made a cup of coffee. The tiled scullery was cold in the early morning. He drank the coffee quickly, and went upstairs for a coat. When he left the house, he could still see the car, a white speck on the coast road.

He caught the first train to the city. It was empty :

the workers' train left an hour later. Paul snuggled up in a corner by the window, and watched the sand and the sea spread out below him, beyond the woods. The sea was peaceful, and there were only tiny ripples around the rocks. Here and there, a long line of water raced out to sea.

When the train reached the city, Paul walked quickly through the streets, where the traffic had just begun, and the shops were opening up.

He stopped at the bridge which overlooked the docks. The ship was easy to spot, for it was the only one that was leaving that morning. There was a cold stillness in the air, and the smell of oil and tar, and food from a coffee stand near by. Behind the docks, a black hill was outlined against the sky, and in front of it the funnels of the ships rose into the air.

A man came up to Paul and stood beside him. He was shabby, and his face was dirty and lined.

"It's a beautiful sight, isn't it, son?" he asked.

"Yes," said Paul quietly, "I could watch it every morning of my life."

"I do," said the man.

Paul turned up the collar of his coat, and huddled into it, to protect himself from the cold.

Paul came downstairs early on the morning when his examination results came out. His mother was talking on the telephone when the postman came. Paul took the letter, and went with it into the kitchen.

When Mrs. Anderson came in, she said immediately, "Bryan McKenzie has run away from home."

Paul was shocked. He had not seen Bryan since the day of the funeral, and he had almost forgotten that he was going to run away.

"Did he leave a letter?" asked Paul.

"Yes," said Mrs. Anderson, "he said that he was going to sea. That's all. Mrs. McKenzie is in hysterics."

"No doubt," said Paul. "Mother, I've passed my examination."

"Did you get a scholarship?" she asked.

"No," he said, "my marks were just good enough to get me into university."

"Oh, well," she said, "we'll manage somehow."

"Aren't you going to congratulate me on passing?" he asked.

"Of course," she said. "You did quite well."

Paul went up to his room, and sat down by the window. He lit a cigarette with unsteady hands. For a while he gazed out to sea, then he picked up a book, with the poem that he loved:

"Even now,
  I mind that I loved cypress and roses, clear,
  The great blue mountains and the small grey
    hills,
  The sounding of the sea. Upon a day
  I saw strange eyes and hands like butterflies.
  For me the morning larks flew from the thyme,
  And children came to bathe in little streams."

But I have never been happy, thought Paul. At least, just for this summer. And it ended.

The cigarette smoke smarted his eyes.

The ships at sea sailed into the distance, reached the horizon, and disappeared.

GMP books can be ordered from any bookshop in the UK, and from specialised bookshops overseas. If you prefer to order by mail, please send full retail price plus £1.00 for postage and packing to GMP Publishers Ltd (M.O.), PO Box 247, London N15 6RW. (For Access/Eurocard/Mastercharge/ American Express/Visa give number and signature.) Comprehensive mail-order catalogue also available.

In North America order from Alyson Publications Inc., 40 Plympton St, Boston MA 02118, U S A.

NAME AND ADDRESS IN BLOCK LETTERS PLEASE:

Name...

Address...

....

....

....